ISBN [978-93-341-4977-7]

Table of Contents

Dedication for The Silent Choir

To the voices that have been silenced,

the hearts that have been stifled,

and the souls that have been lost in the noise.

This is for those who dare to reclaim their sound,

to find harmony in their individuality,

and to rise, even when the world demands their silence.

May you always sing your own song,

and may your voice never fade.

With gratitude to those who have inspired me,

and to the community that shows us we are never truly alone.

— Manpreet Bhatti

Preface to The Silent Choir

In a world where one's own voice is drowned by the cacophony of numerous voices, it seems that individuality is something fragile to lose or at least hide under layers of expectation, conformity, and even fear. The Silent Choir came from the belief that each of us carries a voice to be heard, a story to be known, and a unique light to shine in the darkest spaces of our existence.

The journey of this book will be of Layla, a character who has been molded by hardship and victory, as she sets out for the fight against an overwhelming force: The Choir, a metaphor for all the systems and beliefs meant to suppress the humanity in each of us. Through her, we'll find what fighting for autonomy, finding one's identity and recovering hope even in oppressive cultures means.

The Silent Choir, at its core, is a story of transformation-personal and collective alike. It grapples with unit versus individualism: one can be part of something greater than oneself without ever losing themselves. The struggle for freedom that we see in Layla's story is matched by the strength that comes from embracing vulnerability, connection, and the power that a shared purpose can bring.

For anyone who has ever felt overwhelmed by the noise of the world, for anyone who has doubted their place in it, for anyone who longs for something deeper, something meaningful, and something that gives life a strong sense of purpose, this is to remind them that no matter how silenced they may feel, our voices do matter-and when we stand together with truth, it becomes a harmony more powerful than we could have ever imagined.

I encourage you to join Layla on her journey of exploration and, through her, to discover your own voice within the pages of The Silent Choir.

Episode 1: Echoes of Silence

The room was heavy with sleep and dust, and only the morning light struggling in through the curtains could suffice to illuminate. Layla's small apartment adorned with the morning shallow shadows on the floor. The dust particles in the room was spinning in circles with the luminescence, just like the particles of a galaxy.

Layla opened her eyes and the mist lifted from before her eyes stumbling upon the fact that she was still within the confines of her personal space. The walls were a pale blue with magnificent paintings – some of them quite detailed, some of it just the remnants of the artist's thought process. She frowned at the sketchbooks that were thrown on the floor like the yellowing leaves, as each page gave evidence of the effort she had so powerlessly made in her effort to turn her feelings into art.

She slowly got up from the bed clothes and her black hair flew free and fell up to her shoulders. As she proceeded to go to bathroom, Layla get to see her reflection on the mirror. That conjuring glower that suggested sleepless nights grappling with creativity were indistinctly etched beneath the eyes. She inclined on the table, raking fingers through her scalp, as if trying to untangle her ideas.

The warmth seemed to extinguish the darkness she felt inside, though the light on her skin was unable to chase the sadness on her soul. Her last art exhibit seemed as though it was from a lifetime ago, a lifetime where she had caught pains that followed her stroke. Layla had a vision of standing before the audience; she could still hear a distant sound of clapping. It was as if each piece was her so much so that she could not know them anymore, at least not versions of her that she put on to perform for The Choir, but sanitized reflections that reflected the views of the latter.

With a heavy breath she swung round and looked at the mirror then she stepped towards her easel and the empty canvas staring her in the face. She took the paintbrush and it brought her the familiar feel in her hand. There was a desire for something to change – that today wouldn't be the same in her heart for a second. But as she looked at the white canvas that was in front of her the burden of expectations was the sheet on her creativity and suffocated it. On the colours of her paints there was only laughter now which only pierced her soul reminding her of the feeling she had lost – the feeling she could not find again.

Layla then placed the brush back into the holder with a capitulating kind of huff. She had to walk, she wanted to leave and get out. Maybe Café Resonance would give her the drive she so much needed In the first place.

"Layla reached the café"

The little bell on the café's door swung as Layla entered Café Resonance, the smell of roasted coffee welcoming her like a long lost friend. The fountain of discussions in a café was the resonance of guests' thoughts to be heard through The Choir. Layla opened her eyes and clearly experienced awareness of surroundings; the pulse of the crowd seemed suffocating to her.

This was designed to give everyone the feeling they are at a lively restaurant with friends chatting and engaging passionately about the latest trends. The women felt touched when Layla experienced a twinge of envious – a sting, a signal that she was alone. shifting her focus to the barista himself, she wondered whether today will be routine; the same order she makes every other day; a caramel macchiato.

"Good morning, Layla! The usual?" The barista smiled, and Layla nodded, offering a weak smile in return.

"Yeah, thanks."

Snippets of conversations were kicking her around, all of them creative and connected, as she waited for her coffee. Another table was buzzing on about a collaborative art project while another table was talking about a new musical composition. With warmth and camaraderie each shared thought rang, but for Layla it only expanded her feeling of being apart from everyone.

Returning her drink, she found a tiny table in the corner to soak in the noise. She set her tablet down, opened a digital canvas. She began to sketch with a flick of her stylus, but the ideas would not hit her stylus, slipping through her fingers like water. The strokes were forced, the pressure to build mounting with every moment that went by.

Only her laughter from the table near her had a dull roar in her ears like her silence, speaking among the collective voices. Just then, Maris, her best friend, joined her, a radiant smile brightening her face.

"Hey, Layla! Mind if I join you?" Maris asked, sliding into the chair opposite her.

"Of course not," Layla replied, forcing a smile that didn't quite reach her eyes. She dreaded another conversation about her reliance on *The Choir*, but she didn't want to alienate Maris either.

It was harmless, yet the weight of her insecurities always seemed to sink in when she was around Maris and her plans for the day: As she went about talking about her plans for the day, Maris shared her ideas for an upcoming art showcase with a captivated air.

"You know, I've been thinking that we should work on something together, sometime." I feel that unique style that we could map together."

There was a knot in Layla's chest. "I don't know, Maris. These times have been rough, I've been struggling to find my voice. "The noise is even like I'm lost."

Maris concerned eyes shone. "It's funny because you have such a different perspective." Why do you let The Choir drown it out?"

The words struck a nerve. The Choir helps ... Layla's frustration boiled over with a retort: "The Choir-helps us ... connect..." That's how I can tell people my thoughts."

"But at what cost?" Maris pressed, her voice rising with urgency. "You're losing yourself, Layla. You need to break free and find your own inspiration."

The patrons of the café nearby felt the tension coming and began to shift their attention. She was embarrassed, the anger mixing with the flush of her face. Her voice sizzled with hurt, she snapped, "You don't understand."

"The Choir is all I have! And it keeps me from feeling isolated."

Her resolve festered, but her expression softened. You would just want her to be happy. I'd like to see you make something that's all yours."

But all the Layla could do was feel the walls closing in, and the weight of expectations laying on top of her. 'You may just have to go,' she murmured, before she could pull it back.

In reaction, Maris suddenly stood up, scraping her chair against the floor. "I can handle that." I can't let you let The Choir define you!I can't watch anymore! She stormed away with that, and Layla sat there at the table, her heart pounding in her chest.

The cheerful racket of the café dropped to a murmur, and Layla stirred her untouched coffee, spinning the caramel below. Yet watching others sipped away their words and emotions, they read their posts with a laugh filling the air. Her isolation seemed to grow further and further apart from the collective, with times magnifying that gap.

She stood abruptly up, moving the chair along on the floor as she made the decision to walk out the door. The sunlight outside hit her like a wave; warm, inviting, but far away, mocking. She relived the argument with Maris, and was reluctant to reach out to apologize. But her silence was itchy wanting to be revealed and gnawing at her, with whispers that it may be time to embrace it.

She walked aimlessly through the bustling streets of the city with a heavy heart. Each step felt like a weight lifting, the world around her only made her turmoil worse. She glanced down at her phone watching people post their digital art on their platform. On her last post (a piece she'd been proud of at first), her finger hovered. Against her insecurities, it seemed small.

In that mind blurring moment of clarity they realized they were lost, in a world that valued compliance over truth. An art supply store caught her eye just ahead of it, its windows inviting her with colors and textures that spoke to her creative soul. Layla took a moment to catch the smell of paint and old canvas, an old friend she recognized again.

She breathed in deeply and made her decision. Time had come to feel out her own self, to break free of The Choir. With a push of the door to the store, Layla ready to take her voice back again and set herself a new way to go, no matter how long it took for her to find herself and the world again.

Episode 2: Whispers in the Dark

Layla's footsteps echoed softly on the damp pavement as she made her way through the quiet streets of her neighborhood. As always, The Choir was at that soft hum in her mind, the late afternoon sun hung low, casting long shadows across the ground. The content of everyone else in range was familiar, comforting, yet distant, ever familiar and comforting because it was a constant reminder of the world she lived within. But today something felt different. Layla's focus was somewhere else though, and the usual chorus of thoughts swirled around her.

She let her mind drift, her feet going vaguely where they had to go and the thoughts of others floating over her head like background noise. She had her own quiet discontent she was caught in, listening without. Another day, another walk home, another day that proved to be another day of failed inspiration. It was dry as the creativity she knew once felt surging through her veins. She had not known that her art was hollow, disconnected; she knew that her last exhibit had been met with polite applause. Everything had felt like it was supposed to live with The Choir, not her. She wasn't a creator, only a conduit.

The steady hum in her mind cut suddenly, leaving only silent sound. There was nothing for the briefest moment. A black, empty, hollow quiet, no voices, no emotions, no shared thoughts. Blinking in confusion as she stopped in her tracks, Layla said nothing. Her pulse quickened and she looked around. The shops were closed, the street was empty but that wasn't the vagueness in her mind. The Choir never stopped. Not like that.

Her heart beat faster. Was it just a blip? A momentary glitch? But, holding her breath, she waited, but soon the familiar hum returned, filling her again. But the unease lingered. Layla sighed in relief. Telling herself it was nothing. A little technical glitch, a little lapse in the connection. But as she continued walking, the sense of something being off clung to her like a shadow.

Layla walked past a vibrant street mural, a sprawling, colorful community art, whose uneasiness increased. Today, the mural usually looked full of the life and energy it exuded the day before but today, it looked odd muted. Oranges and blues were brighter and more vibrant, now, and seemed duller. She looked up, stared at it as though the paint had faded in a single night itself. She blinked, her throat tight, remembering that maybe she'd imagined it, or that her connection to The Choir was starting to bend the world around her.

She shook her head to get rid of the discomfort. It was just a glitch. Come on, Layla, she told herself to get over it. But as she turned away from the mural, the thought lingered: Was it really just a glitch? Or am I the one having some kind of problem?

These thoughts that came in from The Choir seemed a lot different than before. Bursts of ideas—pups of a moment's passing, then silence. In gaps that hadn't been there before. Layla shivered. Something was wrong with The Choir, but something was wrong with the world she always knew.

Reaching her studio, the unease had turned into full blown anxiety. Today, the small space was oppressive; usually filled with light and creativity inside. The air was dense, air sticky with some intangible thing. Stacked everywhere, were unfinished canvases but half realized ideas lay on the floor in a mess of brushes, palettes and discarded sketches. A half finished landscape glared at her from far wall, a reminder of her failure to finish anything, like art.

Layla dropped her bag onto a stool, and in front of the blank canvas she had set up days ago she hoped inspiration would hit. It hadn't. The strange silence on her walk home made the thought of creating something almost impossible.

Picking up a brush, her fingers trembling just a little as she put the brush in dark, stormy brush, blacks, grays, and deep blues. Her hand moved as if driven from something deep and restless, inside her. The painting it left behind was as if a storm had come crashing just over its mural and the brushest strokes just hovered across the canvas in broad erratic ones. Violent waves crashed against each other, swirling clouds began to form in the dark sky and streaks of lightning cut through the sky. Her heart was pounding as she painted feverishly about her confusion and fear, about putting the puzzle together, about not really knowing what was going on.

That storm wasn't a glimpse of what the world was outside. It was her. She could feel the chaos in her mind, the frustration, the feeling being lost essence coalesced into the dark, tumultuous scene in front of her. Each stroke freed the unease, but each movement brought with it worse. She stared at the storm she had created, then stepped back, hands on her chest as she heaved. Her hands were shaking as if they were holding a paintcan. It seemed alive, swirling and churning not only on the canvas, but within her soul.

For a long time she could stand there and stare at it, trying to understand each emotion inside her. It was a growing sense of dread, her chest worsened with a knot in it. She wiped hands on rag, glancing around round room as if the walls would all close in on her.

Suddenly someone buzzed her phone inside the tense silence. She jumped, and fumbled for the device. That was a notification from The Choir. Her fingers were trembling, so she hesitated before opening it. When she finally did, the thoughts and emotions of others began flowing into her mind once more, but something was different. The thoughts were distant, muted, like echoes of what they were usually, of their being. Layla's breath quickened as she realized it wasn't just the earlier glitch. Something deeper was wrong.

The storm mocked her but she looked back at her painting. Was she slipping away from the rest of the world? Was she just out of sync from all the crap that was going on in her own chaotic mind? Everything had become unclear: the lines running between her inner and outer worlds.

As Layla cleaned up for the night, preparing to leave the studio, she heard it again—the silence. It was faint, just on the edge of her awareness, but it was there. This was was not the silence of peaceful solitude, but a hollow emptiness, a hollow eerie absence, like The Choir and her connection were beginning to fade, to slowly thin at the edges from each other.

She stood still, straining to listen, but the silence dropped off as quickly as it had come. She looked back one more time at her storm-filled canvas to the swirling darkness, her fears painted upon her, matching the canvas. All of the glitch, the silence, the storm… all felt like they were connected, like pieces of a puzzle she wasn't ready to solve yet.

She turned off the lights and set off, into the night, with a growing sense that her world was spinning away from her, with a heavy heart.

Episode 3: The First Note

Layla was wrapped around into the night in a blanket of false comfort as she drifted into an uneasy sleep. They were used to the hum of The Choir at night, she had learned to sleep through it. But tonight was different. It always started out the same: disjointed fragments of thought, of no meaning and shape. Although the landscape solidified and she was walking through a place she had never been before. Her feet were heavy on the ground, the air cloying with the smell of spice she'd never known. There was a mini bustling marketplace around her, strangers moving in a blur and their faces indistinct, but their presence overwhelming nonetheless.

Wandering through the market, layla brushed her fingers across the rough texture of one of the vendors cart lined with woven baskets. Suddenly, the world lurched. She wasn't Layla anymore. Her hands weren't smooth like they used to be, not anymore, they were calloused, aged, the hands of an old woman whose spent her life laboring. The dream fragment in flashes of other lives.

An anxious mother, her eyes glued to a child who was quite far away and fear choking inside her. She was an artist then, no, this artist was frantic, putting paint on a canvas with reckless abandon, hurried strokes that were wild and crazy. The dream changed yet again and now Layla was a man standing at the edge of a cliff and below him the roaring expanse of the sea, he rolled his shoulders back. She could almost hear the man's thoughts reflecting in her mind, his despair so intense she could see it suffocating her. Each life was so vivid and each identity so compelling that she sank further and further with each new one into lives that weren't hers, lives more real than can be cleanly dismissed as dreams.

Panic clawed her neck as her breathing quickened. She didn't know where she started and where these people stopped. The vision grew more and more visceral, more and more terrifying. Her heart stuttered as if it would explode and Layla gasped for air. She finally jolted awake, sweating, drenched in sweat. Her chest heaved, she blinked furiously, trying to dislodge the residue of the dream washing back to her consciousness. Replaying the fragments in her mind, she couldn't help her mind as it searched from fragments for some unseen meaning. What had she just lived the lives of?

Morning came, though the light make its way through her window yielded no reprieve. That heavy weight of those dreams pressed down on Layla, who sat up. The strangeness of it all had begun to show; the vivid lives that had played before her eyes this morning clung to her like shadows. Today, The Choir's soft hum was faint behind her ears. Her eyes remained fixed out the window, checking the street below, the world still moving around her. The fog in her mind wouldn't leave her thinking about the strangers' lives.

Making her way to the kitchen layla stood up and her steps were heavy. It was the same smell, the same warmth of a mug clutched in her hands, but it was the morning routine, the grounding one that usually drew her in, which wouldn't comfort her today. She felt like an outsider instead of a spectator, not as part of herself. She started to sip on the coffee, but it wasn't that flavorful, there was no comfort in it, being bland. She practically looked like a duller version of her world.

The dreams asked her questions to gnaw at her. Are they memories? What am I living in these people's lives, in my sleep? Her felt like it was unravelling her sense of self, once solid. She couldn't shake the feeling that her individuality was slipping away, replaced by the lives of strangers she couldn't place. With every minute that passed, the world around her felt less familiar, her connection to it weaker.

Weary, Layla retreated to her studio, hoping the process of creating might help her reconnect to who she is. She felt empty, she felt the usual peace and refuge of her art went missing as she came into the room. The once sanctuary studio now became suffocating. An amplification of the dissonance in her mind, the silence of the room pressed down on her. On a blank canvas she stood, brush in hand, but her usual creative flow refused to come.

And she watched the pictures in her dreams—a mother seized by anxiety, a painter thrashing to his brush, a man at a cliff's edge. Her own face was blurry, but her sense of strangers was perfect. With an aimless and hesitant drag the brush across the canvas. They were forced up every line, as if this wasn't hers. Only the unsettling sense of loss with her work only deepened the disconnect.

The lines on the canvas were indistinguishable. The brush was hurting her hand, as surely as if a flame was grasping her hand with the force. The dreams weren't her dreams, not hers, and they fractured her mind, trying to scatter her. She threw the brush down, the brush clattered around in the empty room, as she was frustrated. It was so quiet it felt oppressive, like it wasn't just the room holding its breath waiting for her to admit there was something so very, very wrong.

Layla moved toward the large mirror, hanging on the far wall, feeling the walls of the studio closing in on her. Her reflection stared back at her, and she stood before it. But something was off. At first she didn't know what it was, but soon as she stared her own face, she could feel a creeping unease overtake her. Her features were maybe not quite the same. For a fleeting moment, her eyes didn't look like her own. Her mouth seemed foreign, unfamiliar.

Her heart pounded in her chest and she stepped closer. Blinking, she hoped that illusion would pass, but she could feel it growing. In that split second, she wasn't looking in the mirror. And she panicked the surge, instinctively reaching up to feel the face. The reflection went back to normal, but the fear stayed. The question hung in the air like a threat, she whispered to herself. "Who am I becoming?"

"Layla fell away from the mirror and her heart still raced." Part of her needed to get away from this and the feeling of losing her. She pried her eyes shut and attempted to tap into The Choir, trying to psyche the familiar comfort of the collective. Yet it wasn't the warm hum of shared thoughts, it was a distant, fractured The Choir. The connection - it was weak, distorted. The usual flow of ideas and emotions, feeling for her, reached deeper, try to clutch at it, but what she felt was broken, incomplete.

The Choir was dissonant, the voices, garbled, fragmented. Instead, the clear stream she was used to was distant echoes of the thoughts of the others. Her pulse increased at the disconnection in Layla's mind. Holding on to The Choir like it was the only thing that could make her feet touch the ground again, she grabbed at it more and more, until it slipped further and further out of her reach.

Trying to block out the now hollow, broken noise with her ears, she failed to realize it wasn't coming from outside. The silence wasn't in her, it was around her. The one place where she had always assumed that The Choir would stick to her side, that she wouldn't find them gone without a fight, without chaos, without discord… was slipping away from her; she was alone in a silence that was as terrifying as it was absolute.

Layla sank into a chair and her hands trembled. All that's left to hold onto is a ghost of what it once was: The connection to The Choir. That stream of shared thoughts and comparative creativity had drifted away to the point of being faint echoes. Now her own existence felt more like a figment of her imagination, whereas the vivid dreams: they weren't stranger's lives. Looking at the half finished painting on the easel, a chaotic, no direction in sight, muddled colour mess, she did. It was a painting with no purpose, just as were her thoughts.

Layla knew that she couldn't grab at straws anymore — that inspiration was no longer real. It was too deep: disconnected from herself, from her art, from The Choir. Her trembling hands reached for her tablet, her link to The Choir and she cut it off. The silence that followed did not come a moment too late, a huge empty void knocked her back into the room and pressed in on her.

Layla was alone, for the first time in years, no longer shared thoughts, no reciprocal consciousness, just Layla and she could suck it. The decision hung heavily in the air and she stared at the canvas. I may need to loosen this connection so I can find myself. Still the thought terrified her.

Resonance of Fear   (Layla's sudden disconnection from The Choir)

EXT. LAYLA'S NEIGHBORHOOD – DAY

Layla walks along a familiar street, the noise of the city blending perfectly with the hum of The Choir in her mind. Faces pass her by, but she doesn't see them. Her thoughts are (sang together well/worked together well) with the total (of everything or everyone) awakeness/awareness of the world around her.

LAYLA (V.O.)
(reflective, calm)

The Choir... it's everything. People, the voice of one humanity, a world that has come to terms with itself. An environment in which ideas, intentions, and free air exist in a single union . Who can now even dream of living without it?

As she strolls, she nods at a neighbor on a walk without even needing to look that direction because she is completely encased in The Choir now. The neighbor just looks at me and grin, meaning that they see me as part of the whole that connects them and me.

Suddenly breathless LAYLA falls and her eyebrows crease as the voices fade. A very low electrical hum breaks the chain of group ideas.

LAYLA (V.O.)
(confused)
What was that? A ripple?

The voices of *The Choir* stutter, then... SILENCE.

LAYLA's footsteps stop mid-step. The silence is crushing, like the world has gone *deaf.* She reaches out mentally, but there is nothing. Her hand presses to her chest instinctively, her eyes wide with shock.

LAYLA (V.O.)
(panic building)
What's happening?

EXT. SIDEWALK – DAY

Still on the pavement , LAYLA topples in place and concentrates with all her might to reconnect to The Choir once more. She attempts to contact and her respiration becomes restless seeing that she is not able to feel anything. Her thoughts are scattered.

She then puts her eyes shut, and does not move at all as she concentrates even more. People walk so close to her and she gets more agitated thinking of what is likely to happen next.

LAYLA (V.O.)
(focused, desperate)
Come back... please, come back.

Her lips move as she *whispers*, trying to coax the voices back into her mind.

LAYLA (whispering)
Come on... come back...

Nothing. Just suffocating, dead silence.

Suddenly she wakes up and she can hear the throbbing of her heart. His breathing accelerates she becomes disconnected to her environment as her focus becomes myopic. Her gaze darts from one passerby to another, looking for any sign of shared panic.

EXT. BUSY STREET – DAY

LAYLA looks at a group of people that is walking across the road. They slide around, their faces serene, related. He sees how delicate they look while smearing, how they speak the things which they no longer say.

LAYLA (V.O.)
(fearful)
Are they still connected? Is it just me?

She steps forward and tries speaking aloud to a MAN passing by.

LAYLA
Excuse me, can you——?

The MAN doesn't stop. He walks past her without a glance, as if she's invisible.

LAYLA (V.O.)
(helpless)
No. It's just me.

Her heart pounds faster, her sense of isolation growing. She's a ghost in a world full of the living, her presence unregistered by the collective mind.

EXT. STREET CORNER – DAY

LAYLA pulls her tablet out of her bag, her hands trembling. She fumbles as she unlocks it, scrolling quickly through her contacts. She tries sending a message to one of her friends.

INSERT – TABLET SCREEN:
Message: "Are you still connected? Please answer."

The screen flickers. No response. Her hands shake as she taps the screen again.

LAYLA (V.O.)
(anxious)
It's just a glitch. They'll answer. They have to.

She checks the digital feed, hoping for news—an outage, a system error, anything to explain the severed connection.

INSERT – FEED:
Empty. No messages, no updates.

LAYLA's eyes widen in horror. She types another message, this time more urgent:

INSERT – MESSAGE:
"Can anyone hear me? Please respond."

Nothing. Just the cold, unresponsive silence of her device. She feels her chest tighten.

EXT. SIDEWALK – DAY

LAYLA starts walking nervously all over the place. She moves swiftly, her breathing is short. She hath her fingers on her temples, rubbing them as if she might try to force herself to remember The Choir on the impotent mass of grey matter between her ears.

LAYLA (V.O.)
(*spiraling*)

Why can't I hear anything? And, then what if this is indelible and what if in future it is irreversible as well? What if I am like this, frozen like this for the rest of my life?

Her mind is faster than her legs as she paces around frantically touching emptiness while wishing for stillness. Her eyes get cloudy for a few seconds, the loneliness constricting her airways.

LAYLA breathes heavily and her faces turns red this meaning she is on the verge of having a panic attack. She utters a scream, her hands trembling and extend out to touch a YOUNG WOMAN that is passing by.

LAYLA
(*frantic*)
Help—please, can you hear me?

The YOUNG WOMAN walks by without acknowledging her.

LAYLA's panic rises as she spins, desperately looking for someone, anyone, to recognize her, to see her.

LAYLA (V.O.)
(*overwhelmed*)
No one... no one even sees me.

EXT. ALLEYWAY – DAY

LAYLA's pace quickens as she leaves the crowd behind, seeking solace in a quieter space. The lady moves to a small dark lane away from the noise of the city at a very alarming pace, full of nervous energy.

Her body shakes, her mind screaming in silence.

LAYLA (V.O.)
(desperation turning into clarity)
If I can't reconnect, if *The Choir* won't take me back... maybe I'm better off alone.

She fears, but her determination to retreat slowly begins forming in her mind as she walks through the alley. Instead, she departs for her studio — the only place where the girl can at least attempt to function without the added weight of the world on her shoulders. She turns and begins to walk down the alley and with every step she takes – she moves a step closer to the unknown life.

INT. LAYLA'S STUDIO – DAY

I gasp and sit up as LAYLA comes striding into her studio, her chest rising and falling from the intensity and the door slamming shut with finality. The door closes and she is suddenly all alone encased in this huge metal box with bars on the windows. She presses herself agains the door, her back rigid and straight; her face white and her eyes opened wide and staring.

Inside the studio, it is particularly quiet, and this silence can really feel quite lonely.

LAYLA turns her head to the room that the organization provided her as safe haven but there is no warmth found there. Her studio, once a place of refuge and creativity, now feels like a tomb. She moves forward; she starts walking to a canvas placed close to the wall with a window.

LAYLA (V.O.)
(resigned)
I'm alone. Truly alone.

She reaches out and touches the canvas, her fingers trembling as they brush against its blank surface. The act feels hollow. Empty.

LAYLA glances out the window, watching the world pass by, knowing she's no longer a part of it. She turns away, walking deeper into the studio.

LAYLA (V.O.)
(determined)
If I'm going to find myself again... it has to start here. Without them.

She sits down at her workbench, her hands resting in her lap. The silence inside the room is deafening, but for the first time since the incident, she breathes deeply, accepting it.

LAYLA (V.O.)
(softly)
I can live with this. I have to.

The screen fades to black as LAYLA sits in the silence, alone in her thoughts, facing the new reality of life without *The Choir*.

Episode 4: Call to Adventure

Layla moved cautiously through the city square, burdened as the waves of people circled her, dancing to the straight face of The Choir. It was to be a day of happiness, a rally that should have been used to showcase success stories of the link that held society together. Individuals hummed and whistled and people as they spoke and performed, and feeling through, and communicating through, The Choir. Projected on the square several screens displayed selected visions of the collective success-scientific, individual joy, and above all, the age of miracles that The Choir had been promising.

Everywhere Layla looked, faces beamed with the glow of connection, their features serene, as if nothing in the world could be more perfect than being linked in mind and spirit. It is important to know that to the crowd, this was everything. A harmonious world. A society where people could just get each other or receive information without having to explain to other person's concept about everything.

Layla felt none of it.

As she was dancing between people, carefully stepping on cobblestones she thought she could hear and even feel the thoughts moving around her, electric spark of thoughts connecting people. But none of it touched her. The connection that once hummed in her mind was missing and what had once been a familiar glow that of a night lamp was now frigid as watching a fire from behind the layer of ice.

In front of her a woman raised a baby, the faces of both beaming with happiness while they said something through The Choir, the baby's laughs mixed with her quiet chuckle. Layla's heart clenched. It was not that she was seeing the union; she no longer belonged to a world of shared consciousness. She had been severed from it.

The more she stayed, the stronger feeling of emptiness inside her became. She flinched, and looked the other way. The very square which used to be a home seemed like another planet inhabited by people whom she couldn't possibly comprehend. The Choir, which once embraced her with its combined minds and togetherness, was nothing more than a symbol of all that she has been deprived of.

Layla was checked out, and it showed in her stiffness. Her actions were robotic, shivering shoulders as if she shielded herself from a flurry of thoughts around her. Each smile, that is each joy or sharing of laughter and even a mere indication that people are communicating and relating deepened the loneliness in her flesh. She walked as if a world was on her neck and she was choked; that is how oppressive loneliness felt to her. The more she tried to push through the crowd the more lost and isolated she felt suffocated by the lively spirit of the celebration.

Then the noise began to swell.

With the onset of some what as the sound of a whisper; the buzz grew louder. Layla came to a stand still, she was choked as the people's thoughts around her were vivid throughout the scene. Even though she was no longer associate with The Choir she was still capable of feeling the strength of the choral assemblage. It pulsed against her head, a cacophony she could not comprehend or turn a deaf ear to it.

People started swaying together with different rhythm, which reminded one of a specific organism. Layla's heartbeat quickened. The noise in her head, boomed through her auditory system, constant, unending, but none of the voices were her own. She tripped, instantly raising her hands to her ears though the sound was not real and coming from around her. It was all pervading and absent, a background noise of voices she could not shut out.

"Stop," she whispered to herself, but her voice was swallowed by the growing roar.

The world around her blurred. The faces of the people began to alter in her eyes, their faces contorted the more her anxiety level increased. She refused to let herself hyperventilate… Layla placed a palm on her heart and felt the surge of tension that felt as if it emanated from the inside of her – her heart threatening to explode any second. The celebration that she received has become a nightmare — a clear manifestation of the unity she no longer possessed.

She shut her eyes and tried to relax, tried to breathe, but it turned into a panting microphone belonging to her chest. Even when she attempted to focus her mind and get her bearings the split persisted. She was alone. A stranger in her own city.

Growing increasingly claustrophobic from the very sound of happiness, Layla hurried out of the square and past cheerful people. Her legs took her to the less boisterous part of festivities where the dance, cheers and merrymaking lessened. It was a short stint of freedom in the middle of hurricane.

And then she saw them.

There were several individuals distant from the remaining people, they had a rather stern look on their faces. They did not dance to the beat of The Choir. They remained motionless, immobile just like when they were during the noise in the demonstration. Then suddenly Layla stopped as she directly looked at the group. They were not a celebration – at least not in the same way as the others. He saw it in how they stood, how they stared with a lack of passion. They, too, were disconnected.

Her curiosity piqued. Without thinking, she took a few cautious steps forward.

They were men and women of different ages, dressed simply, posturing tensed. A particular man was somewhat apart from the others, quickly glancing through the happy people and then at Layla. His gaze rested upon her, with kind of a steely determination in his eyes – as if he suddenly know her and she know him in some special intimate manner that had changed their dynamics.

Despite her determination, Layla's feet started moving towards the group – closer to them. But the feeling that tormented her – and that she could in no way shake – was a sense of being wanted, of fitting in. These people were like her. Disconnected. Lost.

And so as she got near, an older woman moved forward. Her eyes sunk deep in her head but burning with a fiery conviction; her face lined with sorrow. The intensity of her stare they made Layla hesitate but she did not slow down.

Her voice was sweet and authoritative when she decided to speak. It drowned the faint sounds of the revelry from the other side of the hall behind them.

"You feel it too, don't you?" the woman asked, her words heavy with meaning. "The silence… the emptiness."

Layla swallowed hard, her throat tight. The admission caught in her chest, but she nodded. She did feel it. The silence had become her constant companion.

The older woman looked at the others and shook her head as if she realized well the predicament they were in. "You're not the only one," she said, and she could feel the bitterness seeping through her. "We were once part of it. Just like them. But now… we're nothing. Were buried together with the remainder of the world, isolated from the only head that controls them all.

The others nodded and the faces showed the suffering that was clear in Layla's face.

For the first time since her disconnection, Layla didn't feel entirely alone.

Something in that woman's words resonated with a part of her inside which she tried to quell, similar to what Layla felt. There was loneliness, frustration, the feeling of rejection of a greater whole in their eyes. The same thing had befallen them.

"How?" Layla's voice was barely a whisper, but the question carried the weight of her confusion and desperation. "How did this happen?"

The older woman shook her head, her expression sad. "No one knows. One day we were connected, the next… gone. Like we never existed."

One man in the group stood up, an old, tired looking man who looked as if he had not eaten in days. He growled, "It's like being erased." "In one sickening second you are apart of the world and then the next – not anymore. The next, you're a ghost. No one sees you. No one hears you. Even people you care for… they glance at you, but it feels like they're seeing through some invisible wall.

A young woman a lady who seemed to be in her twenties raised her voice and said something that sounded more like a whisper. "I lost my family," she said. Taking any chance they have to ditch me is something they do without hesitation 'They don't even notice I'm gone.'

Layla's heart ached with each story. These people were reflections of her own life experience and they were hearing and believing what she had to say. The more she listened the more her mind raced. Why had there been this disconnection? Just a technical glitch in the process, or it was by design?

She felt her minds going round and round as the accounts accumulated and grew heavier as more stories came to her. If this had happened to others, if they were all shut out of the world for no reason, then there had to be something more. Knowledge they lacked, information they were never being given.

Much as they seemed to stare at each other, neither of them spoke as the silence lacuna filled up questions unvoiced.

Layla turned back to the older woman, her voice firm despite the uncertainty swirling in her mind. "Why?" she asked, her words cutting through the stillness. "Why are we being cut off?"

The woman shook her head again, her face etched with sorrow. "No one knows. But we need to find out… before it's too late."

Then response in the woman's voice was so determined, it made Layla feel something deep within her. The amount of fear and confusion that she had felt since the disconnection finally started to make way for something else in her mind – determination.

The way that Layla saw, the Silent's, around her and the way she saw that she could not go on living like that anymore. Isolated. Cut off. She needed answers.

"I won't live like this," was voiced more as a murmur in the company of comrades than addressed to them. But her voice grew stronger. "I'll find the truth."

In that case, for Layla, there is nothing left to do but to continue pursing her dream. She had to practice what she never understood before—reality, for herself, for the others and for the many still connected beings who may also end up like them one of these days.

The journey had begun.

Episode 5: Breaking the Silence

The city lights flicker against the evening sky as Layla steps onto the busy street. The buzz of voices and the ideas discussed in The Choir never ceases, it buzzes like the heartbeat she used to find reassuring. Now, it's like static; loud destructive noise, up in front of us and beyond our control. She stands in the doorway of a café where everybody she is friends with is hanging out, watching them chatting and laughing since their minds are one. Her heart pounds in her chest as she stays there unmoving, hand on the doorknob.

It is mirthful inside, electrifying the area with the spirit Layla no longer has the capability to reach out to. She has friends at a large table, and in the dim light it is clear that all of their faces are animated. She inhales, exhales and opens the door to enter the warmth of people chattering away. Suddenly, it is if the water has risen up to her chin—the clamor and buzz in her head is nearly deafening, and none of it is including her. She clears her throat and steps toward the table helplessly, attempting to smile when she gets near him.

"Hey, Layla!" Sarah speaks out and her voice is warm but detached at third person. Layla simply gives a jerk of her head, and lowers herself between two of her friends, the sound of their laughter grating on her ears though she feels as if she is alone. Another is she sees them exchanging ideas with words which they do not say in a silent conversation from which she is excluded. She watches as they share thoughts silently, a wordless exchange that she is no longer part of. The invisible wall between her and the networked minds of her friends is palpable.

Layla feels her breath getting caught in her throat as she listens to everything that is happening with increasing speed. It moves around her and she is a distant passer by, observing the flow of words and feelings at the table but being unable to touch them. She clings to the armrests and forcibly reminds herself that she is in the twenty-first century, not in a burning building.

Hoping to drown her own voice she is barely heard, she manages to ask: "So, how's everyone been?" Her friends look at her for a second, nod or make a half-smile in her direction before returning instantly to the conspiratorial conversations which The Choir has now become for them.

"Everything's great!" Sarah grins and responds: Well remember we have been working on the new project you discussed here, and were all involved in the process. It's really coming along."

Layla nods, her throat tightening. "That's… good."

The words taste hollow. She knows she was once part of those brainstorming sessions, once deeply integrated into their world. It is like having a companion but now the discussions as good as belong to a different universe. The hum of The Choir is a ticking clock with the memory erased of who she is, of a mind shared that is no longer hers. Her friends' thoughts are bubbling up from one to another while she is trying to fit into the network, which she cannot join.

Sarah looks a little tense as she shifts closer and drops her volume. "Layla, don't worry. It's just a phase you are going through. You'll be back with us soon."

Honestly, all that Layla can do is fake a smile in response – her stomach is churning. Nevertheless the words coming from Sarah's mouth are said to soften me but instead they are a barb. The world around her is changing, leaves are falling, while she is being left stagnant and pushed further away from the life she use to live.

In the evening, while Mark spends the evening sitting in the same café, Layla is across from him, and the hum of the city breathe through the walls. She stirs her coffee absent mindedly, looking intensely into the dark liquid as her mind does. Mark is one of her oldest friends, someone she's known for years, someone who, before her disconnection, she could always count on to understand her. But even now, there's a distance between them that Layla can't seem to bridge.

Her voice is breaking slightly because, she says, 'I just don't know how to cope with this anymore.' "It's like I'm invisible. No one sees me, but I'm standing right there. No one hears me. I actually don't exist in their world anymore," it's like I don't exist there anymore.

His brow furrowed, Mark listens. He leans forward to the table, the elbows on the table, trying to comfort her. "Layla, I get it. It actually sounds tough, but it's probably just a phase. It takes some time, and you'll come back."

The mug in her hands clenches with Layla's grip. "It's not just a phase, Mark. "It's not a trend that's going to go away." When she looks at him she wishes for a bit of empathy to pass over his face, to identify the true depths of her suffering, but his face has imploded and she sees only the emotions of those he uses to connect to The Choir. The weight of her own isolation weighs heavier now, like the first punch to the chest. You've got no one, even the people closest to her can't explain the void that she's trapped in.

Hours later she's back in the quiet of her apartment, sitting in front of a blank wall. The silence in the room is suffocating and she can't ignore the constant inevitability of absence, of The Choir neglected ache. Her trembling fingers reach for her tablet now, her scroll taking her to old photos; images of her and her friends, laughing, connecting. Each photo is like a window into a world she has no ability to get back to.

Tears blurred her vision as she looks at smiling faces on the screen. The full weight of that disconnection hits her chest, and her hand drops to her side as the tablet falls from her grasp. She can't stop the decay of the life she had, the friendships that she loved.

Soon now, the tears come streaking, uncontrollable sobs shaking the body, curling up on the couch. She's never felt so alone, never so completely cut off from everything that used to be her whole. It's silence pressing from all around, suffocating her, reminding her that she's become isolated now.

The next day Layla stands in front of her friends again, her heart beating harder against her chest. She knows that she can't keep this up pretending and going on who is normal anymore. As we speak, her hands tremble, her voice shaky but it's firm.

"I need to tell you something," she begins, her throat tight. "I can't do this anymore. I feel like I'm disappearing. None of you… none of you really see me anymore."

Other than herself and her friends who look awkwardly at her, all face looks confused and uncomfortable. Her voice is gentle, but patronizing, and she reaches out. "You're just Adjusting, Layla." You'll find your way back."

Layla shakes her head, her frustration boiling over. "No, you don't get it. I'm not coming back. This is my life now."

These finality laden words hang in the air. Her heart is beating, but Layla turns and walks away, knowing she has pushed them further, but also knowing they never had a chance to start with.

Layla is alone on the street, watching herself withering in a shop window as The Choir's public announcement flashes by on the screen nearby. The reflection mocks her with smiling people's faces connected and happy. As she stares back at her, her own pale, hollow face looks back at her; a shadow of who she was.

Again she tears up, but not this time do she draw tears. Instead, her face becomes hard and her fists actually clench at her sides. She isn't going anywhere without the world moving on. Not yet.

The suffocating silence pressed in upon her once, but it is different now. There's a void she could fill with meaning, there's a space.

Context :

It's not emptiness. This space she can fill with her own purpose. Layla — slowly — understands that if she can't go back to The Choir, she'll have to find a new path to live on her own.

Her reflection stares back at her with quiet determination.

Episode 6: Pull Out Rug

Layla made her way down the dark coloured street to her usual hard of the evening, the evening air remained incredibly still. All day the weight of the disconnection from The Choir had been heavy on her mind, but this night's atmosphere felt off in a way, the city seeming to choke on its breath. As she walked her thoughts swirled again in a familiar haze of loneliness, the constant sound of her footsteps bouncing off the quiet looking buildings.

As usual, the café was bustling, but there was The Hum of The Choir there, although obviously invisible. Around her, the connected believers behind her continued, smiling and nodding with that strange sense of everything perfectly aligned. Layla felt all the familiar pang of isolation and looked around the room — her eyes landing on a group of Silvent people in the corner.

This was different tonight, tense and charged. Layla approached and picked up on bits of their whispered conversation, her eyes went cold with worry. The one said, 'Maris is missing.' "Days that no one had heard from her."

Layla froze. But that wasn't all — Maris was one of the few Silents she'd connected with in this disconnected world, and he'd vanished? It had been weeks since she'd seen her friend, but she hadn't had this kind of gap between them. Layla's chest had been coiled in fear and the knot became tighter. The Silents were becoming something dark, but it had taken her a moment to realize just how high the stakes had become.

Layla's apartment was suffocating that night; it wasn't just normally silent. Her bed was watched by her, as every shadow in the room seemed to pulse, with something that wasn't there. The quiet was always something she had hated, but it was different, and she could feel the silence watching her, waiting.

Restless and overwhelmed with the tension in her mind she got up and darted to the window. Down, the city lights flickered and long, distorted shadows danced across the streets. Every person they marched past, every heartbeat, their fingers switching from keys to fretted strings as they carried on through the city, was connected: moving with the same ease, same synchronicity that The Choir allowed. What they knew not was all, what lurked just beneath the surface.

Layla couldn't stop thinking about Maris though. Where had she gone? Why would she disappear? What could it be, something The Choir had done? The questions whirled, louder and louder, with every tick of the second. Layla squeezed her fists and there was an intense feeling of deep paralyzing fear in her gut. What if Maris was taken, and could she be next? She thought, and a wave of cold terror swept through her. She had to do something, anything to protect herself.

Layla didn't let the soft glow of her tablet illuminate what she was doing the next morning: sitting at her desk with a determined expression. Hesitation gripped her fingers just briefly, as she lifted them toward the screen before she plunged in to her research. The Church seemed always omnipresent, but how much did she know of its influence? If Maris's disappearance was directly related to them, she had to know the truth.

She read article after article, each describing The Choir's wide spread reach of control over the government. The deeper she went, the more and more detailed the details became. Anonymous Silents warned of unexplained disappearances, as well as sudden mysterious deaths. It was hard to tell fact from paranoia, but the threads wove a tapestry of sinister undertones.

Then, a post caught her eye. A Silent, who said they had been targeted by The Choir, told it to me. The post read they know we are a threat. "We don't 'set records' — we don't break records, they can't control us so they silence us in other ways." Layla's pulse quickened. Maris's disappearance wasn't a coincidence—it was part of something much larger, something terrifying.

Later that night Layla went down into a basement of some old building sitting out on the outskirts of the city. Silents usually kept it discreet, it was the place where the dead, or as we called them, the Silents could meet and communicate with each other in any which way without being watched. The Silents' whispers in tones that would have made even the deafest cringe filled an otherwise dark space with a nervous sheen.

The eyes in the room settled on a small group near the back. Coming up to them, she knew them from before but not terribly well. She spoke, her voice just a bit strained and steadier than I've ever heard her.

There was tense silence, and she said, "We have to find out what happened to Maris." "She's not the first to go Silent." We have to find out what is The Choir hiding."

Elena stepped forward, a woman with sharp eyes and a serious expression. She'd heard of her, Silent, a woman with a name for distrusting The Choir. Elena's voice was low but firm. Anybody who's not falling with the flow is being silenced, and The Choir's control is growing." Maris is just the latest."

Layla's breath caught in its throat. Elena confirmed her worst fears. Their killers weren't so isolated; they were being hunted.

Two days passed and Layla stood outside of The Choir's Public Office, sleek glass paneled headquarters her heart banging away in her chest. That was risky, too risky maybe—but she couldn't back out now. Layla fitted herself in with the crowd of Choir people as they made their way into the building by using Elena's false identity credentials, a motion with every movement an attempt to stay unnoticed.

The headquarters was sterile, if efficient on the inside. The connected ones moved in their silent ways undeterred by Layla's presence among them. She made her way through the labyrinthine corridors, her palms slick with sweat as she approached the secured room where The Choir's internal network could be accessed.

The soft hum of technology filling the air when Layla swiped her ID card and was able to step in the flutter-focused room. Tapping away busily on the terminal of The Choir's database, Layla quickly placed herself behind the keyboard and hacked. It was only a question of time as to when it will be noticed. She was not about to rest until she discovered what happened to Maris.

With a flicker, her screen displayed a file with the caption 'Disconnection Protocol'. As soon as she saw what was under the caption, Layla almost choked on her breath as her mind registered the horrifying reality.

Layla's expectations of what the Disconnection Protocol would entail could not have been further from the truth. They had been tracking the Silents for a while now, and the Choir had been branding them as threats that needed to be eliminated. Maris was among a number of people who's names were removed along with some dozen others, marked 'For removal'.

Trembling hands were all Layla had left with after such emotions of such a nature sank in. This wasn't merely an issue pertained to dominance; it was a question of extirpation. Midnight began to conform on one basic principle; that was absolute order and nothing less than that. Everyone who could challenge that order was to be eradicated. It wasn't just that Maris had vanished. No, she had been removed, has in being taken to be eliminated from the records.

Betraying weak knees, Layla backed away from the terminal and all that was left was a very rapid heart rate that made mere sitting down impossible. The others needed to be informed.

Episode 7: Shadows of Dissonance

Layla stood at the edge of the dimly lit room, her back against the cool cracked wall. The basement air was thick with an unspoken tension, a sense that hugged every silent figure within it tight. They were all acutely aware of the danger of their presence here, for should The Choir's enforcers find them, it could kill. But desperation had sent them underground, grouping silently in secret beneath the city's surface, the only sanctuary that existed from The Choir's omnipresent control.

The crude assembly muttered low words, but as a figure stepped into the room, the whispers died away too soon. Layla followed the shift in attention, her heart pounding. A man entered the dim light filtering from a solitary, flickering bulb. His appearance demanded instant silence. Theo.

He stands calm in a way that's unnervingly so; his shoulders square, eyes raking the room as if he could see into the heart of every Silent. Every movement is measured to the point of being almost considered. Theo's poised confidence stood in stark contrast to the restlessness of the group. Layla couldn't tear her eyes away as her stomach twisted into knots of uncertainty.

Theo began to speak, his voice flowing smoothly yet firmly. "We come together here because we refuse to be controlled, to allow our thoughts to be dictated by the will of The Choir. They would have us believe that connection equates to freedom, but we understand the truth. We recognize that connection is merely their instrument to monitor and suppress. Maris. Maris understood that truth as well."

And at the mention of Maris, a weight settled over the room. Layla's breath hitched. Maris had been one of the few voices who'd ever really questioned The Choir before she was taken. Nobody really knew what happened to Maris. Everybody suspected the worst. Theo went on, his words sinking deep.

"They are targeting us. Anyone who resists-anyone who chooses to stay Silent-is a threat to them. But we are more than they think. We are more than just individuals disconnected from their system. We are the last defenders of free will."

Layla listened, completely captivated. Theo's words resonated within her, bringing to the surface the doubts she had buried deep since Maris's disappearance. Yet, as Theo's eyes roamed across the room, they landed on Layla. His gaze lingered there a heartbeat too long, and in that fragment of time, Layla felt an unsettling exposure, as though he could see within her: her uncertainty, her fear. And yet, in that look too was something more: a recognition, as though he understood the turmoil that stormed inside her.

Layla quickly shifted her eyes away, but the moment had already passed. The meeting drew to a close, and the crowd quietly melted away, each individual slipping back into the shadows from which they had emerged. Layla lingered near the exit, her mind still swirling with thoughts of Theo's speech. She found herself uncertain about him. Was he the leader they so desperately needed, or merely another influence attempting to draw her into something she wasn't prepared for? The prospect of trusting anyone now felt perilous.

Before she could slip away quietly, she was made aware of a presence beside her. She turned to see Theo standing there, his eyes steady. "You came," he said, with a gentle authority.

Layla swallowed hard as her mind whirled with how to respond. She hadn't expected being noticed, let alone being spoken to directly by him. "I. I wasn't sure if I should," she confessed.

Theo's face softened. "Leaving the shadows is never easy," he said. "But, Layla, I can see you are made of steely stuff".

She felt like her heart skipped a beat. How did he know her name? Her bewilderment must be fairly obvious, because Theo smiled at her, a small, almost reassuring smile. "You've been through a lot," he said. "Maris's disappearance-it's shaken you. I've seen it happen to others. But we can't let fear rule us. We have to stand together".

Layla felt a tightening in her throat. She yearned to trust him. Theo radiated a confidence that made her feel as if he could steer her through the tumult, assisting her in uncovering the answers she so desperately sought. Yet, an unsettling whisper of doubt lingered within her. "I don't know if I'm ready," she admitted, her voice scarcely rising above a whisper.

Theo tilted his head slightly, studying her. "No one ever is," he replied. "But when the time comes, you'll know where you stand."

With that, he withdrew, leaving her solitary in the dimly lit room. Layla observed his departure, her thoughts swirling with a mix of uncertainty and hope.

Yet the cool night air contrasted sharply with the oppressive warmth of the basement. Layla huddled her coat tightly around herself as she walked through deserted streets. And yet, with every step she took, an escalating sense of unease coiled in her stomach. Something did not feel right.

A slight sound, barely perceptible, caught her attention. Footsteps light, cadenced, two dark shapes ahead of her advancing in step. Layla's heart beat fast. No need to glance around to realize who they might be. Choir enforcers.

They wore black, fitted uniforms, silent even in their actions, yet somehow incredibly powerful. Trained to recognize Silents, to track them down, and "reconnect" those wayward souls to the ledger of The Choir, no matter what such a soul wanted, Layla's heart thundered in her chest as she quickened her pace, forcing herself to stay calm. Maybe they hadn't found her yet.

The hum grew louder, closer. Layla's breath was caught in her throat. She ran around a corner in a hurry and saw a narrow alley. Without hesitation, she slipped into the alley, flattening herself against the wall, her body quivering with fear. The mere murmur of some of the enforcers' communications drifted through the air-uneasy in its precision. Her breath was halted, hoping in vain that they would not enter this avenue.

The minutes stretch, becoming what feels torturous seconds. The humming fades out as the enforcers moved on, their cold, staccato movements carrying them deeper down the street. Layla breathes out again, her knees shaking with relief.

She ducked into a small shop nearby, the door creaking softly as she slipped inside. The shopkeeper was an old man with tired eyes, but he looked up and met her gaze without saying anything. He didn't need to. He was one of their kind-one of the Silents. Layla nodded her thanks, and in response, the shopkeeper gave her a knowing look, then disappeared into the back.

For a second, Layla stayed there, her hands shaking from the close call. She had been perilously close to being caught. If the enforcers had seen her, it was all over. The seriousness of the encounter champed down on her chest. She knew she could not stay hidden in the woodwork for long. The Choir's influence was growing by the day, and it was getting better at finding those who chose to fight back.

Days passed, and Layla conflicted. Theo and the Silents offered her a path, a way to fight back against The Choir's control. But every step she took toward resistance put her in greater danger. The Choir's enforcers were always lurking, and the safety they promised was tempting.

One day, while roaming the city, Layla stopped in front of a massive digital billboard. The Choir's propaganda glowed intensively; no need to be a genius to know what was clearly written: "Connection Equals Freedom. Join Us, and Never Be Alone." The faces of those who had joined filled the screen, where wide smiles spread and eyes burned with satisfaction.

She let herself imagine what it would be like for one of them: the pleasure of surrender, of never running, never fighting, just. belonging. So easy. And yet, with the imagination as fleeting as a nanosecond, Maris came back to her—the way she vanished, all those unanswered questions. The freedom The Choir offered was nothing but an illusion, and Layla knew there was no going back.

Later that evening, she met with Theo again. They sat in a small, candlelit room, far from the prying eyes of The Choir. Theo's usual charm had faded, replaced by a grim seriousness. His eyes locked onto Layla's, and his voice was low, almost a whisper. "The enforcers are closing in, Layla. Maris's disappearance was just the beginning. You're in more danger now than ever."

Layla's chest tightened. She knew what the risks were, but somehow it felt very different coming from Theo. "What am I supposed to do?" she asked, her voice barely stable.

Theo leaned back, his features unreadable. "You have to choose, where you'll stand with us. We need you to fight. But if you're not ready, they will find you. And they won't be kind. The truth dawned when Layla sat there, as Theo's words still loomed in her mind. She could not stay in the shadows anymore. The time for indecision was over. It was time to either fight or fall.

Episode 8: Chorus of Doubt

The room's dim light flickered as if it were listening to Layla's breathing rhythm. She is sitting cross-legged on the freezing floor where a dozen other Silents sit, one completely absorbed in his thoughts and the other doing the same. In the center, he stood tall and gathered himself with a flawless self-control, imposing without ever saying a word. The air feels intense; Layla cannot describe it. She had begun to trust Theo in those past weeks, yet the tension that filled her when he was near had only intensified. If anything, it had grown sharper.

"The first step," Theo began, his voice low but steady, cutting through the thick silence, "is unlearning what The Choir has forced upon you."

Layla closed her eyes as instructed, turning her attention away from the murmuring of the city outside. The weight of the outside world pressed against her mind, but she knew better than to let it in. Theo had explained that this training was necessary-essential if she was going to stand a chance at resisting The Choir's influence. The Choir's manipulation wasn't just societal; it was personal. It seeped into every dark corner of her mind. Warped memories. Twisted truths. Made her question what was real.

"Focus," Theo's voice came again, sharp this time. "Find yourself beneath the noise."

Layla took a deep breath, seeking the stillness within the turmoil. Instead, recollections slammed against her mind-impressions of her childhood warped through The Choir's training. Her mother's face stared back at her, followed by her father's, then. Maris. A shard of pain pierced her chest as the figure of her closest friend materialized in her head, her face indistinct, her voice muted.

Maris. The reminder of her disappearance almost broke Layla's concentration, but she held on to the exercises, digging tighter mental fingers into herself. Theo had told them: The Choir would use everything against them, including the people they loved. Layla had to keep her head sharp, reclaim those parts of herself lost beneath layers of manipulation.

"Reclaim your mind, Layla," Theo's voice cut through the haze, as if he knew the desperation. "It's yours. Not theirs."

Something clicked. A jolt of clarity. Layla felt a memory-real and unvarnished-rise to the surface. It was foggy, a trail of a childhood moment shared with her family, untainted by The Choir. For a split second, she was just Layla again, before the rebellion, before The Choir had taken over.

She opened her eyes, panting. Theo was looking at her. His eyes had smoothed over to a sheen. He nodded once. It was a gesture, a recognition of the small victory that she had gained. It was draining and enlightening. She started to claw at the identity The Choir had taken from her.

"This is only just the beginning," Theo said quietly, addressing the rest of the group.

Later that evening, after the group had begun to disperse, Theo approached Layla. "There is something else you need to see," he said more seriously than he had since morning. He led her further into the bunker. a section she had never been in before. The atmosphere changed because the walls were narrower, colder, and seemed heavier with more oppressive air.

Theo stood before a great iron door, his back to her. "The maze," he said flatly. "You will have to go through it alone. No one to guide you, no one to assist you. Rely on nothing but yourself."

Layla's stomach turned over. She had heard rumors of this trial but did not believe she would come up against it so soon. "What's inside?" she whispered.

"Your mind," Theo said. "And The Choir's tricks. Nothing is real, but everything will feel real. It's meant to confuse you, to make you question what's real and what isn't. Your work is easy: get out of here."

The door creaked open, opening onto a dark, winding maze of narrow corridors. Theo laid a hand on her shoulder. "Remember what you learned today. Trust yourself. No one else."

Another nod to herself, Layla stepped into the cold, oppressive labyrinth, her heartbeat increasing with each step. The door slammed shut behind her, sealing her in that condemned place. The overhead lights flickered, casting long, eerie shadows on the walls, making it difficult for her to discern what was real and what wasn't.

As she marched further in the maze, familiar ripples of thoughts started twisting, errant echoes of hoarse whispers coming from unknown distances. Some whispered doubts; others misled her. She clutched only to Theo's last words, trusting her instincts over everything else. But the farther forward she ventured, the louder the whispers became, changing her course in every direction.

"Layla… help me," a voice called out. Her heart froze. It was Maris.

She turned around, her eyes wide. There in the dim light stood Maris, her face pale and desperate. "Don't leave me," Maris begged her voice cracking.

Layla's eyes welled up with tears. She'd been searching for Maris for so very long, hope against hope that she'd still be alive. Yet a thing in her chest twisted painfully—it wasn't real. Theo had warned her.

"I… I can't," Layla breathed, forcing herself to look away from the illusion. She struggled with every little bit of strength she could muster to move her legs forward, away from Maris, away from the past she wished she could change. The illusion exploded behind her like shards of broken glass, leaving only the cold, empty corridor.

At last, what seemed to be hours had passed when Layla finally emerged from the labyrinth, her breath shallow, her body trembling. Theo stood at the exit of the labyrinth watching her with an unreadable face. His gaze was still awhile before he opened his mouth to say, "You are stronger than you think."

The following morning, Layla sat in the cramped below-grade room lit by the dimmest of holographic maps and data displays. Theo stood at the head of the group, surrounded by a small circle of trusted Silents. They were planning their next move: an operation to expose The Choir's darker side to the world.

Theo ironed out a map of the central facility for The Choir, where their neural experiments were conducted. "Here's where they institutionalize control," he said, his voice hard. "Advanced neural implants to suppress free thought and enforce loyalty."

Layla listened closely to the other Silents and their stories about The Choir's brainwashing techniques. Each story was more horrific than the last, but Layla's resolve only grew stronger.

Theo sighted his gaze her way, his eyes burning with intensity. "Layla, we need someone to infiltrate the outer perimeter. With your new mental focus, you're our best hope of not being seen."

The weight settled heavily on her chest, but Layla nodded anyway. The mission was dangerous, but she felt ready. For the first time in her life, she felt like she belonged to something bigger than herself, something that could potentially bring real change.

Theo took Layla aside after the strategy session to hone the training to an even deeper degree. They sat in cross-legged position in a silent room, with Theo leading her through the process of generating a "mental shield": a barrier between The Choir's neural scans. Layla's mind ran amok with doubts, but it was Theo's soothing voice which grounded her.

"Focus. Think of a fort around your brain. Nothing can penetrate."

Earlier, it seemed impossible. But as she focused her mind, a slight hum at the back of it — the incessant monitoring by The Choir — began to recede. When Layla opened her eyes, Theo was slightly smiling. "You're ready."

Later that night, Layla crept through the city's underground tunnels with heart racing, senses guiding her to The Choir's facility. She flipped the switch on in her mind and felt that now-familiar hum of their scanners probing the air, for a moment becoming invisible to them.

Then, out of nowhere, a group of enforcers emerged, their high-tech scanners far more powerful than she had ever anticipated. Layla's shield buckled but she gritted her teeth and steeled herself with all she had learned from Theo. She powered the barrier back into place just in time, scooting into a side alley as the enforcers began to file down the street.

Panting heavily, her heart racing, the mission had now proven more dangerous than she'd ever assumed.

When Layla came back into the bunker, she stopped in front of Theo. His face was pulled tight with anxiety. "You're taking it too far, Layla," he whispered. "The Choir is gaining power. Their scanners-what you just fought off-are only small beginnings."

Layla's pulse was still pounding from the hand-to-hand, but she steeled herself. "What do we do?"

Theo's eyes grew cold. "We fight smarter, not harder. But if you slip up, even once, they will find you. And once they do, there's no escape."

His words had hung heavy over her mind. The rebellion had never felt so dangerous. But failure was not an option.

Episode 9: Earning Respect

Layla crept low through the shadows, her heart beating steadily, as she went for the nerve center of The Choir. Her black suit clung to her form, camouflaging her in the darkness. Nothing stirred but the slight hum of The Choir's automated defense drones zipping by. Theo's words still played in her head: This is the most dangerous mission yet, but you're ready.

She hadn't always believed that. For the longest time, Layla had doubted herself, wondered if the fractured remnants of her past, the pieces of her identity that The Choir had stolen, would ever be enough to help the rebellion. But after surviving the labyrinth trial and earning Theo's trust, something inside of her shifted. She wasn't just a Silent anymore. She was Layla-stronger, smarter, and more determined than ever to bring down the system that had tried to erase her.

At the facility's perimeter, the air was heavy with tension. The towering walls of the building were sterile, metallic, and cold-just like the organization they protected. But Layla was ready. Her mental shields, taught to her by Theo on how to craft them, were up and hiding her presence from the neural scanners that could have picked up on her. It was a delicate balance, trying not to let those shields drop even as she moved rapidly and stealthily in the dark, but Layla had perfected this. She had to.

Layla lifted her head to the ceiling, breathing slow and deep. She let herself relax against the wall as she concentrated on the patrol drones overhead. Weeks studying these rotations. That's the gap: ten seconds. She moved, fluid footsteps silent across the corridor floor, ghost-like in the aisles of locks. Dodged the first layer of protection.

Inside, it resembled a maze of empty, hollowed-out halls. Layla's chest constricted the more she drew near to the data core, the room protected by the most sophisticated systems in surveillance technology. That was where The Choir's central nervous system was housed. In those servers, the dark testaments would lie—a repository of files that counted manipulation of memories, rewrites of personal history, and complete erasure of lives. It was these files she needed; this was the key to exposing it all.

Her hands trembled as she connected a small device to the security panel, breaking the encryption on the system. Every tick of the override process dragged on interminably. The door slid open with a soft hiss to reveal the interior chamber, illuminated by the eerie glow from the data core.

Layla worked fast, fingers swift in the delicate insertion of another device into the hub as she initiated the download. The holographic display flickered, the screen filling with lines of encrypted data. Her pulse beat in her ears as the download percentage crept upward. 20%. 50%. 80%.

The unmistakable sound of footsteps echoed from the corridor. Layla froze, her heart leaping up into her throat. She had a patrol, and that sent her plunging back into the shadows, her mental shield wrapping tighter around her consciousness, hiding her from view. The footsteps draw closer with those heavy boots clicking on tile in an deliberate rhythm.

Holding her breath, she didn't move an inch as the enforcers walked by; they didn't notice a thing. They didn't stop and look her way even. Layla's mental shield held. Once they were out of earshot, the data transfer completed with a soft chime. She withdrew the device and slipped it into her pocket, then slid quietly out of the chamber.

The mission was accomplished. She now had the evidence, and she had done all of this without ever tripping an alarm.

In the underground bunker, there was a painful sense of tension. Layla stepped in, all eyes on her like an anchor pulling her down. Theo was at the very center of the room, with Silents on both sides. They had waited for her return, unsure if she would succeed. As she approached the holographic display, she saw the indecision in their faces—a mix of doubt with hope.

Not a word was spoken as Layla went to the console and inserted the data chip she'd pulled off. The display came to life, filling the air with documents and visualizations that described the methodology of The Choir. The revelations were worse than they imagined: family members erased from existence, memories of childhood rewritten, entire lives gone.

The group fell quiet. Layla had discovered something overwhelming; information that would have raised eyebrows then, but now proved the faces staring at it with awe. A jumble of some form of pride and fear was building inside her, something neither of them had ever accounted for.

Theo stepped forward, his big hand on her shoulder. His face was somber, but something, a quiet respect, lived inside his gaze. "You did it," he said low and not quite satisfied. The others nodded, their skepticism giving way to approval over her bravery.

It was the first time she felt the burden of her own success. She had earned their respect-this time, not only for finishing the mission but showing them the truth, for proving that she wasn't a liability but an asset. She was one of them now.

Now, when the others were gone, Layla was left only with Theo. The atmosphere between them was charged with tension. Layla had thought that the worst of the job was done; now, however, in Theo's eyes, doubts stared at her as though radiated from within.

"It is good," Layla declared reassuringly, but Theo's jaw is hard.

"You're sure?" he repeated. His voice was steady enough, but there was a flicker of uncertainty there. "We can't afford mistakes now, Layla with something like this".

There was a tangled unease in her belly. Had The Choir known this was going to happen? Had they let her take the data? Her mind was spinning with insidious doubt seeping into her brain. But Layla straightened her spine, lifted her chin, and met his piercing gaze. "I did everything right, Theo. I played by the book".

Theo strode forward, his voice easing in its tone but not lessening in its resolve. "This isn't about the plan anymore. This is about being prepared for whatever comes next. We just declared war."

Layla's heart was racing, but she stood firm. "I'm ready," she said firmly.

Theo looked at her for what felt like a long time before nodding slowly. "Good. Things just got a whole lot more serious".

The Silents reconvened once again just shortly thereafter, this time for a planning session. Layla sat among them once more, not on the outskirts but as a main player within the group. The holographic display showed the major locations of key Choir facilities and, to this network, the memory manipulation network. Theo presented the plan: a coordinated action to damage The Choir's data hub.

Layla's work was crucially important - she had to lead a team into the facility to disable the neural scanners, thereby opening the window for the rest of them to get in. In the discussion over tactics, Layla added her two cents, suggesting things based on what she knew from being inside. Her suggestions were met with nods of agreement, solidifying her position among the rebellion.

For the first time, Layla felt at home in the Silents. She was no longer a mindless follower, but someone who had a contribution to make toward their underground resistance movement. This finally put her in a position where the stakes could neither be more personal nor higher, yet she was willing to do whatever it took to complete the mission.

Layla was alone in her quarters, staring at the small, cracked mirror in the corner. She hardly recognized the girl staring back. She thought of how many times she had tried to redeem the broken pieces of herself, how The Choir had stolen away her memories and used them to shape this identity. Yet now that everything has come crumbling down, Layla will see her individuality-in her recollections, experiences, and emotions-she realizes her strength.

She was not just a survivor, but a fighter.

Memories of her childhood, of Maris, came flooding in clearer than ever before. She gifted herself a moment to grieve for the life she'd lost-but to really grasp onto the woman she was becoming. Her individuality, once a nervous weakness, now spurred her into determination to bring The Choir to their knees

It wasn't about revenge anymore. It was about reclaiming who she really was.

Just as they were setting their plans, the emergency alert flashed across the bunker. Layla and Theo made a dash for the control room, where the feeds showed a disturbing site—The Choir was mobilizing. Their forces tightened around the security of the facilities.

"They've picked up the breach," Theo said, his voice shadowed by darkness. "They know we're coming."

Layla's mind was racing with adrenaline coursing through her veins. Now this is it-the moment of truth. But she didn't step back. "Then we adapt," she said firmly and surely, "We'll be smarter. Faster.".

Theo looked at her, his face unmoved, but a flash of respect gleamed in his eyes. "You're right," he said, turning toward the rest of the team. "Everyone ready yourselves. The real fight now begins."

As the team adjusted their plans, Layla's resolve hardened. The Choir was going to attack back, but they weren't going to win. Not this time.

She was on the side of the truth- and that is far stronger than whatever weapon the Choir may have brought along.

SECTION BREAK: First Pinch Point - The Silent Choir

There was low light coming from the machinery of the operating bunker, which illuminated the sullen faces of Layla and the Silents as they concentrated at their consoles. Layla thumbed her fingers effortlessly on the console inserting the chip to transfer the data she had risked her life just to obtain from The Choir. They collectively felt the tension of the air, the realization that they were reading something that could tip the tail in their favour.

"Their patterns… they've been quite unpredictable…" Theo grumbled, and scowled at the monitor. He was always the collected one of the gang, the one who could look at a situation and work out what to do without getting upset. But tonight he too was on the nerves. His jaw clenched a little at that last piece of information that Layla presented—a list of Choir targets—those who have rebelled against the Collective in secret.

Layla felt the intensity of the information to her that through her veins and rippled through her mind. Said information, if employed correctly could put a spanner on The Choir's next move, grant them a boost. But she was wise enough to know that she wasn't safe yet. Whether they thought they had planned a year ahead or sometimes even months, The Choir was never far behind if at all.

Suddenly an acute sound of a siren echoed through the room.

Everyone froze. Layla glanced at the surveillance camera screen and immediately she caught her breath. A pale green light from the security lights bathed the bunker interior as the dark shadowy figures in uniform advanced across the screen.

"The Choir's enforcers," Theo whispered angrily, the last layer of the civility slipping of his tongue.

Layla's stomach dropped. They had been found.

"We have no time left," Theo whispered which was in fact very loud and very real statement to make. Layla looked at him and for that one moment of eye contact, she remembered what she was doing here and what they both were doing here. The Choir right to them. There was no escape. Not from this.

It was obvious to the bunker that the approaching enforcers were about to shake it. The rest of the Silents scrambled to prepare for defenses, then in one spin on her heels, Layla snapped into action. Boots thudded along the walls, joined sounding by the mechanical roar of that bunker's steel doors struggling to handle the pressure.

The room was assessed by Layla's ears, a pounding could be heard in her ears as she took it in. Their weapons weren't enough, and the bunker's walls, while reinforced, wouldn't hold out for very long. She thought of their few options.

Against all of the mounting panic, Theo's voice cut through. "Inside, everyone!" Layla, we need time—"

The moment he spoke, the steel doors crash with an earsplitting cacophony that beats constantly. The door opened a crack for a squad of enforcers, pristine uniforms uneasily clashing with the chaos inside the bunker; their eerily synchronized movements frightening as shrapnel flew in all directions. They walked in quietly, methodically, like they had won the war. The presence was suffocating, not mattering what was just beyond the edge.

Commander Elara stepped forward tall and imposing at the front of the squad. Cold and calculated indifference was what she beamed through. Elara though, had the aura of authority, the very presence almost drained the air from the room, she was the leader of The Choir's enforcers. Layla's mental shields responded to the ripple of invasive pressure she felt when Elara's eyes fell on her.

The Silents tensed around them, their bodies vaguely preparing themselves for what was about to befall them. Layla knew this battle wasn't physical.

It never was.

Her eyes were icy, and as she moved, her movements were slow and deliberate like she had all the time in the world. The look on their faces told you exactly what you could expect. The Silents fell into an awkward, strained silence, their eyes swiveling between enforcers and Layla, waiting for the inevitable confrontation.

It droned like this, each word carefully chosen, each phrase deliberate, low, and with quiet menace: 'Layla.' "You and your so called Silents, always arguing, resisting." But for what?" Her voice steady, unwavering, she took another step closer. "Freedom? Individuality? You hold on to your 'separateness' as a virtue. But it's a burden. The Choir offers peace. Unity. You continue to reject it and…"

Elara's words washed over Layla's fingers curled into fists at her sides. His tone was hypnotic, a threat — yes — that was simultaneously a warning, like a dark promise that resistance was futile. It was inevitable that the Collective become a thing.

Elara continued to stare right into Layla's face and said, 'You can't outrun us.' "You can't win against the inevitable and I think that plays a big role in Crying in the Club—the story is about kids growing up in the club that we will never know. You can't win that battle. Everything else has been consumed by the Collective consciousness, and you will be as well. One mind. One purpose."

Layla could feel the weight of Elara's words as she settled deep in her chest for a moment. Or could they fight something this powerful? There her eyes swept across the Silents, their faces pale with fear and some beginning to doubt. It seemed as if she had seen it before: The Choir breaking their enemies, no not by force but by the gentle escalation of hopelessness.

But this was different. This wasn't just a fight of their lives. This was their minds, their very souls, fighting in this battle. She could hear it, hear as the gnawing doubt began to return, creeping in and whispering maybe Elara had a point. Perhaps their fight was useless. Maybe they were too late already.

No. Not like this.

Layla sucked in air and returned Elara's gaze, defiance of cold. Elara's words weren't going to shatter her. She didn't want the doubt to grow.

"It's because we fight," she said with a steady voice that also personified her fear and her determination, "because we believe in something you'll never understand. We believe in ourselves."

She said it, and there was a silence afterwords, a palpable one that still hung in the air, filled with the tension that was always between the two women. But Elara's eyes narrowed not with anger. Only cold calculation. They shifted slightly in the glow of their eyes becoming more intense.

The enforcers moved, as one, their eyes glowing dull, unnatural light, and Elara gave a slight nod. The impact was immediate, the oppressive force of their mental assault came out like an iron vice on her mind. It was suffocating, endless and trying to worm its way into her thoughts, trying to erode the centre of her being.

The Silents weren't ready. Pressure increased and some fell to their knees, clutching at their heads. The death attack overloaded her mental shields, making Layla grit her teeth. Elara and the enforcers were pushing, pulling, stripping away her individuality, making her a part of the Collective, she could feel them.

But Layla fought back. It flooded her mind, her family, her childhood, things that The Choir could never touch. Before they had a chance to crash into her, she used those memories as a shield to anchor herself.

The mental chaos cut off by Theo's distant but urgent voice. "We need to move! Now!"

She pushed against the mental pressure, and created a brief, precious moment of clearing her mind. But that second was enough to let them falter.

She blasted out a single, hoarse: 'Go!'

Theo and The Silents moved, they scrambled to grab what they could and followed Theo to a hidden passageway. Behind them, Layla followed, heart beating hard against her chest as they marched down the narrow tunnels beneath the city.

Episode 10: The Crescendo of Control

An expanse of rusting metal and decaying concrete was the industrial district which lay ahead. The abandoned buildings' shadows clung to them, just enough to keep Layla, Theo and the small group of Silents crowded in the darkness safe. Watching the entrance to the reintegration facility, Layla sat with her senses sharpened to see the only prison known as The Choir's was her breath shallow.

It was cold air biting at skin, but there was tension up her shoulders that made it hard to notice. Watching, they had been waiting for hours. Then, out of the silence, Movement. Layla's heart clenched.

From the fog a group of Choir enforcers dragged someone between them. When Layla saw who it was, her stomach hit a bottom. Kaleb. Layla recognized him despite his face being bloodied but the bruises. A fellow Silent. A brother-in-arms. The fierce spark that she remembered once having seen in his eyes was there, defiant and terrified: but now it flared weakly at him as he fought his captors.

But Kaleb thrashed and his movements were sluggish, they were diminishing fast. The enforcers ratcheted up, twisting their wrists so hard that Kaleb's resistance ended up in tatters. The wheelchair dragged his body between them, as if he were a limp doll, until his body sagged between them and toward the door of the facility.

It was sickening feeling a twist in Layla's gut. Kaleb had fought with her at his side countless times. He was one of the strongest of them, always with a plan and even a smile quicker than anyone. It was a brutal reminder how thin the line was from freedom into submission; to see him like this, powerless and beaten. In an instant, she realized: Any of them could have been it. It could have been her.

Her fists clenched so hard that she was biting her own palms. Forcing herself to breathe, forcing herself to stay still, every fiber of her screamed to charge into the fray, to stop what was happening. Too many enforcers, and they were armed. With no point in heading to Kaleb's aid and then becoming a part of that same end.

Theo's hand came down lightly on her shoulder, bringing her to ground. "Stay focused," he whispered. "We need Intel. We can't help him now."

Layla wanted to scream. But Theo was right. They had a mission. Unfortunately, that didn't even begin to relieve the pain in her chest as Kaleb vanished into the facility, got sucked into the maw of The Choir's reintegration center.

The air inside the building was sterile, heavy with the mechanical hum. The darken corridors nearly swallowed Layla and Theo, their footsteps being barely audible against concrete floor. There was the close, inner sanctum of The Choir's horrors, just ahead. The oppressive atmosphere thickened tenfold with each step for Layla.

He looked to a corner, peered to a brightly lit room through a small window. We listened to Layla's heart slamming against her ribs. Kaleb was strapped to a cold metal chair in the center room. He was conscious, but barely. His breathing labored and his head hung low. They moved around him like clockwork, which is to say choir engineers, preparing their instruments of control. The faces were cold, cold, cold and devoid of humanity.

Kaleb's temples were wired, their ends connecting to a large, ominous sounding machine in the background. She pressed herself against the wall and gripped the edge of the doorway with her knuckles, white. Her mind raced. She had to be able to do something. She couldn't stand there and watch this.

But what could she do? The room was heavily guarded, and the reintegration process had already begun.

The machine came to life with an awful high pitched whine. There were electrical pulses sent into Kaleb's brain via the wires, his eyes shot open, wide with panic. And he screamed, his raw guttural sound piercing any and all silence he disturbed. Theo's grip on her arm tightened as Layla flinched, her body instinctively straightening to protect herself, but she didn't move back.

"Don't," he hissed. "We can't help him now. And if they go in there, we're dead."

Layla's anger and helplessness worked their way into her vision, blurring her eyes with her breath. She heard Kaleb's screams in her ears in every corner of her mind. The machine did its terrible work, erasing the pieces of him one by one, until there was nothing left but a broken husk.

Layla felt her chest tighten as Kaleb's body convulsed, violently. This was more than torture. This was destruction. Complete obliteration of a person as they were.

But Kaleb's resistance eroded as the process continued. His body grew more still, his screams diminished. His eyes went blank and never stopped glowing. The bile rising in her throat, Layla swallowed. She wanted to take the wires off his head, she wanted to rip the machine apart with her bare hands. But she couldn't.

Trembling with fury she turned to Theo. "We can't just watch this."

Theo's face was hard and his eyes were dark. His voice was flat: "We have no choice." "We can't save him. And we can stop this from happening to anyone else."

Layla's heart twisted. She knew Theo was right. She screamed to defy him, to rush in and stop the madness, even if it meant killing herself. This she hated—the cold sense of it all. But she had to listen. For Kaleb's sake. For everyone's sake.

Kaleb's body went still, the machine intensifying; a sickening hum filling the air. Glassy eyes, not focused, searching for something that wasn't there. His mouth mumbled; incoherent, his memories gone one by one.

His gaze fell on her position, and her breath hitched when she saw his eyes, blank; there was nothing, soulless.

The wires had been unplugged from Kaleb's head and the process had come to an end, the engineers stepped back. Kaleb slumped forward, head dangling at the same loose pace, as if his strings had been severed. An enforcer stepped forward, who tilted Kaleb's chin upward in order to sit straight.

Upon hearing that, the enforcer's voice was cold and robotic, "Identification?"

His voice was toneless, '3459,' Kaleb replied. One mind, one purpose."

Layla's blood froze. The Kaleb she knew was gone.

When the engineers left Layla sank to the floor, her back pressed up to the wall. She couldn't breathe. Couldn't think. A trail of silent tears ran aimlessly down her face and her body shook from the weight of what she'd just seen. Kaleb was gone. Not dead, but erased. Then his body was still, but his soul, his mind was all gone.

Theo sat down by her and said nothing. He didn't have to say anything. His presence was enough to ground me. The tears dried on her face and took their nourishment, hardening her heart. She couldn't afford to break. Not now. Not ever.

Theo's voice softened "We need to go." Pulling her to her feet, he offered her a hand. "We can't save everyone. But we can stop this."

The horror had renewed Layla's determination and she nodded. This was not lost, Kaleb was gone, but this would not be in vain. She made a silent vow to herself, to Kaleb, and vow to every one who had been taken Silent.

She would find a way to destroy The Choir's reintegration network.

As they slipped back into the shadows, disappearing into the cold night, Layla's mind burned with a single, unshakable purpose: *The Choir would fall.*

Episode 11: Fractured Harmony

The sound of the safe house door creaked as it closed around the group, which was swallowed in the heavy silence which had taken over. She could still picture Kaleb's empty eyes, staring up at his just before they took him out of her life … before The Choir took him out of everyone's sight and robbed him of free will … before forcing him to follow their bread crumbs … before drowning him in a sea of darkness … before rejoining him to the group … taking him away from her and deleting him from all of their memories … taking him away from them all and wiping his mind clean. It wasn't a death as such, exactly, it was worse. Kaleb still breathed, but Kaleb wasn't breathing any more. In retrospect, they had erased him, hollowed him out until there was nothing left, but a shell, a soldier for their enemy.

Layla's arms were wound tightly against her, standing on the edge of the room, attempting to keep a tremble out of her hands. As they already were deep in discussion, the others—Theo, Iris, Decker and the rest of the Silents—were low, concentrated voices. And they spoke of tactics, of retaliation, of next target in their war against The Choir. Their words barely registered though. Layla churning the image of Kaleb, his blank stare still haunting her gnawing at her composure.

The flickering light washed Theo's face with long shadows and I could see it against the dimness of the room. The way his voice was always calm, commanding. Her stomach tight up with her glance at him. They had gotten Theo for as long as he'd been the leader of this fight, and Theo was always so sure of where they were headed. Right now, it felt like a distant dream to be certain.

Layla stayed outside of the discussion as they talked strategy. Her almost forgotten presence gnawed her, stoking the flames of her growing distrust of herself. This is exactly the people she had risked her life beside, fought alongside, but they no longer saw to be an equal. Every so often she caught a look from Iris or Decker, some barely there look that said, silently, wait for me to crack. It made her blood run cold. How had they always looked at her like that? Had his erasure shaken their trust in her?

Her heart raced. There were smaller walls closing in, suffocating the air around me. Her ears were gritting out a muffled hum into her mind in the form of words and half formed plans. She tried to concentrate, tried to participate, but a sense of vertigo had settled in, almost as though a has dropped out from under her, and she was falling downwards into a bottomless pit of questions.

Layla moved toward the cracked window at the far end of the room in a daze. In the dark outside, the city was silent, save for a distance hum of patrolling Choir drones. She pressed her forehead to cold glass, fogging it up while staring into the void. Her thoughts—it is futile to say—they circled and circled until there was nothing left but a tangled mess of doubt and fear.

She'd never felt so alone. She had always known this fight was worth it, believed in her, in their place among the Silents. But now that she'd seen the damage to Kaleb, she wasn't sure of anything anymore. Could she handle this? She really could keep going since it would be so easy to fall as Kaleb did? It was worse still, and they were already looking at her as weak link, right?

Theo's voice cut through the low murmur of the others, calm, as if nothing had changed, as if nothing had just happened, that shattered her world. It grated on her now. He couldn't be so steady, he couldn't be so unmoved.

Suddenly she asked, her voice sharp: 'What's the plan, Theo?' Walking toward the center of the room, she turned from the window. "What's the real goal here? You are all making decisions without me. What am I even fighting for?"

The room fell silent. There was silence, and every pair of eyes turned to her, and for the first time in what felt like forever there she felt truly seen. It wasn't how she had wanted, but … The furrow in Theo's face deepened; guilt or something buried flickered there. He crossed his arms over his chest and stood straighter.

Theo's eyes didn't meet hers, and his voice was steady as he said, 'We're all fighting the same fight, Layla.' "You know that."

"Do I?" She snapped back, frustrated. Well it doesn't feel like it." Then what are we actually doing, Theo? There was nothing else we could do, we just watched Kaleb being erased," and now you talk about the next mission like nothing, " it's just another day.

A little grade school game

As students, we once played this game in grade school, this game was super competitive but fairly simple to play. My friends simply wanted me to represent them over the internet though, they didn't want to play against one another. This game kind of reminds me of it because there's a spirit competition between the two wizards, and if the wizard wins the duel the spells he performs will help him with his research. "You want to know what it means to be a Silent ?" Theo's voice grew colder, almost dangerous, and lower. "It means sacrifice. That means we can't have doubts, questions. We fight. We survive. That's the only way we win."

His eyes narrowed and he stepped closer. The rest of the group watched, waited as the air between them crackled with unspoken tension. "That what it means to be Silent?"

Her heart was pounding in her chest. Her answer was not what she wanted. "Otherwise what's the point if we lose ourselves in the process?" If we turn into nothing more than them..

Theo's eyes flickered something for a moment; fear, maybe or grim understanding. Finally, he said, "That's the risk we take." "It's just so we don't have to fight for others later."

Her hands trembled by her sides as Layla stared at him. She didn't know if she should scream or cry. His words were not nice, but they said something deep within her, that she feared. Was he right? The price of survival?

She was fed up. Layla turned and just walked towards the deep corner of the room, disappearing into shadow. Replaying Theo's words over and over again her mind raced. Was she too weak for this? Would she break just like Kaleb had?

Her fingers found the crumpled photograph of her younger brother in her pocket. His smiling face in return stared at her, full of life, deprived of the grimness of the world of darkness she had been relegated to. He was why she was to fight, why she did everything. Even that now felt far away.

Her eyes watered as she clinged to the photo, her heart aching with the weight of the mission, the weight of everything she had sacrificed, but which now felt like a labor too great to bear. She should have screamed, run, given up. Then, staring at her brother's face something shifted inside her. Now she couldn't afford to fall apart.

Kaleb was gone, but now others still needed her. Her brother still needed her. It wasn't just Theo's mission. It was hers too.

Layla stood up, fists clenched at her sides and a deep breath. She may not have all the answers, but one thing was certain: she couldn't walk away. Not yet.

She walked back to the group, her posture firm, resolve hardening. She strode up to Theo, who looked up, but it made no impact on his expression. Their eyes met, and for the first time in hours, Layla felt steady, unshaken.

"I'm still in this," Layla said, her voice strong. "But I won't be kept in the dark. Not anymore."

Theo's lips twitched into something resembling a smile, but his eyes remained cold. "Good," he replied, a chill in his tone. "You're going to need that."

Episode 12: The Call for Change

The air thick with the kind of stillness that precedes a storm, the safe house was quiet. Layla stood by the window, staring out onto gray swirl of thoughts in her mind which had settled there over the last few days. She knew something was coming, a truth as time approached. Theo was coming now, toward her, measuring out his solemnity, as a man about to deliver a heavy verdict.

Theo motioned for Layla to follow him to a dark corner of the room, where the other's could not hear them. It was as though he was taking careful, considered steps, calculating the mass of whatever would be spoken. The light flickered too faintly to see anything and cast sharp shadows over his features. The tension rose between them thick and oppressive; air crackling like the air before a thunderstorm as Layla's stomach twisted.

"It didn't just reinforce the power of oppressing people. This is more than that," Theo said, his voice only loud enough to barely be heard but rife with the power of something enormous. He waited, as if drawing the courage to speak the next sentence. "It's more than that. It's... it's a weapon."

She blinked, trying to understand what he was saying. A weapon? Theo's eyes found here's and her heart started to race.

"They've been manipulating us, Layla." All of us. For years. The Choir is not only controlling the present, rewriting the past. They erase memories, alter our emotion, change the way we think... You remember what happened to Kaleb…?"

Layla's throat caught up. After the Choir had gotten to him, Kaleb's face flashed before her eyes, his eyes so bright, his stare dulled to a hollow, blank stare. He was, quite simply, a ghost of a man he had once been, a reminder to anyone who had the audacity of daring to question the system.

His voice turned darker with every word he spoke. "That is what they did to Kaleb is being done to anyone who won't resist." If the Choir erases voices it's not only silencing them, it's silencing them from history. 'And soon those people will not be able to tell what's real and what wasn't rewritten.'"

This put Layla's mind into a whirl trying to believe what Theo was saying. The Choir was not just force of oppression, but a system, a system dehumanizing; systematically stripping them off their individuality, those who would not succumb. It had never happened, every piece of dissent, every act of rebellion gone.

Her pulse increased and the walls closed in on her, squeezing her. "So... what do we do?" It was shaky, uncertain voice.

Theo's expression didn't soften. If anything, it hardened. His eyes impaled through her, and he stepped closer. He told me: "You have to decide." 'No halfway with this fight, Layla.' You're either in—cherry red; or out—you low key walk away. But, you have to know, if you stay, the Choir will find you. Just like they did Kaleb, they will erase you. Where you're supposed to risk everything every moment you stay."

Layla felt her stomach churn. It was a challenge she couldn't get away from and the words hung heavy between them. Nothing came out but she tried to speak. She was racing her mind, her thoughts racing out of control.

Theo's voice dropped low and direct. "If you leave, you can go back to your silent life. You'll be safe. But you'll also be complicit. There is no room for hesitation anymore".

It crushed down on her, the weight of it, a life-sucking force that kept her from breathing. She stepped back, and her pulse throbbed in her ears, as if echoing in response to her heartbeat. She had always known this was going to be a fight, but now, it felt real in a way it hadn't been before. Theo's words cut through her like a knife, the stark reality of her predicament piercing deeper than ever.

What if she didn't have the strength? What if, like Kaleb, she too would be reduced to less of herself, stripped of everything that comprised her. her? She had the most difficult time swallowing; her throat was constricted as terror settled inside her chest like a dense weight.

She gazed out at her to photograph she kept folded into the pocket of her jacket. There she was with the brother of her mother's-a young boy full of spunk and wonder, the very person to whom she'd promised to protect. That was why she'd joined the rebellion in the first place-to fight for him; a future free from the world that the Choir considered theirs.

But that photograph now felt to have had roots in a past life from which memories were fading away. Her hands shook as she gripped the photograph tightly to herself as if holding onto something real within a world that seemed to slip from under her at every turn.

And then, once more in this silence, Theo's voice cut through sharp and unyielding. "There's no room for fear in this fight," he'd said, stepping forward to stand in front of her as his gaze hardened into steel. "Fear is how they control us. It's what they feed on. You can't afford to be afraid, Layla. Not if you want to survive".

His words were a slap in the face, harsh and cruelly cold, no comfort of words available here. Layla looks at him, rage and fear fermenting inside her. How could he be this composed? This detached? Did he comprehend what he asked for from her?

"Theo," she said, but he interrupted her.

I'm not asking you to be brave, he said, his voice softening ever so slightly, though his eyes remained cold. But you need to know what's at risk. If you want to fight, there's no going back. Once you've committed, you're in for good. You cannot run. You can't hide.

Layla's chest coiled tight as the weight of his words crushed her down. She feared clawing up through her, though something else did too—something deeper. A flicker of defiance. She couldn't walk away. Not now. Not after everything they'd been through.

She looked back down at the photograph again, tracing her fingers over the edges. Her brother's face stared back at her, reminding her why she had made this choice. And suddenly the fear wasn't all that overwhelming. It was still there, but it was joined by something much stronger than that—a sense of purpose, of resolve.

"I'm not going to let them win," she said finally, her voice steady despite the whirlwind of emotions inside her. "I won't let them erase me. Or anyone else."

He stared at her for a long time. His face was a mask. Then he nodded ever so slightly, his impassive features relaxing into a look of approval. "Good," he said softly. "But remember—the point of no return is what counts".

Layla didn't flinch. "I'm ready."

Words leapt at them through the air, weighing with all that was ahead. There was no rejoicing over any deliverance, but rather a crushing, uncompromising reality about the battle to be fought. For the first time in an eternity, Layla felt clarity within herself. She had made up her mind.

And there was no turning back.

SECTION BREAK: Midpoint

Stillness hummed with anticipation in the warehouse. Layla stood alone, her back to the cold, chipped brick wall, weighed down by the decisions that brought her here. The Silents—the rebels, who, in the fight against the Choir, had become her family— slept uneasily around her in the flickering light of their forms, just barely visible. So each breath brought them with it a reminder of how fragile they were, how close they always were to the edge of defeat.

But Layla couldn't sleep. Her mind spun, the same questions from the moment she became a Silent, still spinning. And could they really defeat the Choir? Would they even be able to make so much as a dent in what control the organization has over humanity? She removed a small photograph from her jacket pocket and held it out in front of her, worn and faded from an untold number of years that the clear overcoat had been in her possession. That was the only picture she had of her brother, Kaleb, before everything blown to hell. Before the Choir got a hold of him.

He stared at her and smiled in the photograph, his eyes bright with the kind of innocence that now seemed impossible. Losing him had almost broken her, and she'd been everything to him. She'd spent so long as trapped in grief and fear, unable to move past the loss. They all had taken so much from the Choir. She had let herself drown in that loss, and she had allowed herself to feel that.

Now, however, when she looked at the picture, things changed. It felt just as familiar and familiar ache in her chest, changed it into something. Determination. There was the fear of chains once, but it felt weaker and looser; as if she could shake it off. She had always thought of this photograph as a reminder of what the Choir had stolen, but now it was something different. It was a reminder of why she was here, why she couldn't back down. She wasn't just fighting for survival anymore—she was fighting to win.

She slid the photograph back into her pocket and slowly exhaled. The warehouse was silent, which made it charged, alive with possibility. It was peace before the storm and she could feel the storm rising inside like her, waiting to explode.

Layla found Theo bent over a table furrowed browed, concentrating about the next mission in the dead of night. Careful, practiced motions moved his hands across the map, setting out possible paths and reeling the map back to its original state and then back each time. She wouldn't have interrupted him normally, especially not at a time like this, but tonight was different.

"I need to do more."

The quiet passed with her voice as if it was a blade. Theo's eyes narrowed in confusion, looking up. Strategy was rarely moments when she spoke. Layla had never pierced the background, she watched, she learned and she aided from the sidelines. But not tonight. Her jaw set with a newly formed resolve, she showed no hesitation when she passed him.

Then she continued, "I can't just sit on the sidelines anymore, Theo, she said, her voice was still, even she was surprised at how strong it sounded." "I'm ready to fight. "Plus, this is the first time I'm not afraid of them anymore."

He looked at her for a moment and his face was unreadable. Finally he said, 'No, Layla, this isn't a game.' Once you're in there part of the fight, once you step into this, there's no going back. You have to be sure."

She looked him right in the eye and answered, 'I know.' "And I am. We have to take the fight to the Choir, not just the Army. I'm not requesting your permission, Theo. I'm ready," I'm telling you."

And he paused, watching her carefully, and for a moment neither of them spoke. Then, slowly, Theo nodded. "Alright. But this is on you now."

The next morning, a day that was going to be just like was the norm. The warehouse were the Silents would spend the day preparing for another mission. Fatigue written to everyone's faces, tension hanging thick in the air. Theo explained the plan while standing near the back of the roaring crowd and waiting for Layla to stand out and approach. A risky mission, a intel-gathering mission deep inside the Choir's control zone. Today, that wasn't enough; normally she would have blended into the background.

But Layla's voice penetrated the clatter, "I'll go".

Eyes poken open in surprise, heads turned. This was never a volunteer Layla was willing to do something like this. She could feel something change as she met the gazes of her comrades. This is because she had always felt she was uncertain, but now felt she had steely determination.

Her voice was stronger 'I know the area,' she continued. "I can get us in."

Theo didn't hesitate. He nodded and Layla felt proud. This was it. She had left the game and was now a player. The stakes had never been higher, and.

Every shadow was cause to fear it contained a threat in the streets of the Choir-controlled city. Her senses were pruned to a sharpness and her heart bounced off adrenaline like it had been given a damn good shot of TDL. Rest of the Silents fell in behind her to blindly trust her to lead them through the labyrinth of alleys and backstreets.

A group of Choir enforcers approached, patrolling nearby as they made their way through to the heavily guarded data hub. Layla didn't waste time to signal to the others and led them into a narrow alleyway, fading into darkness. They travelled with precision, gliding through the tins city blood like shadows.

Layla allowed a small breath of relief when, finally, they got to the data hub. She had done it. She wasn't just surviving anymore—she was leading, and for the first time, it felt right.

That night later back at the safe house, the sense of rush from the mission wearing off, left Layla by herself, and her thoughts filled her. Standing in front of a cracked mirror she stared down at herself. Doubt as much as pride remained. Could she really handle this? Could she really lead?

She drifted to images of Kaleb, his hollowed erased self haunting her. They had taken him, made him the Choir. But what if she wasn't strong enough to stop them from doing it to others?

He pushed the doubt away, but as the doubt crept in. Her reflection turned hard as she clenched her fists. She'd been ruled by fear too long. She wouldn't let it win now. Because she was this far.

Layla stood at the front of the room the next morning, showing the eyes of the Silents. His arms were crossed and his expression unreadable, but Theo watched it from the sidelines. Everyone waited for her to say something, and when she did her voice was strong and resolute.

Layla looked at each of their eyes as she said we're not just surviving anymore. "They, we're going to take the Choir down." And this is how."

The room shifted as she laid out the plan. They weren't just tagging Theo anymore. They were following her. The waver uneasily to gain control of his weapons, but Layla felt fully in control of her own destiny for the first time.

Episode 13: Mirror Stage

A broken mirror loomed in the face of Silents' hideout before Layla: each piece shattering into her own face. It was a likeness she barely recognized-jagged and disjointed as though every splinter had a different version of herself. She looked at it, tight breaths in her chest. The broken glass seemed sneering, showing her the person she was, not the person she wanted to be.

It was cold in that room, and the silence circling her was heavy. That's just the way it had always been—the silent cloak encasing her like a comfort and a burden all at once. Layla's fingers twitched on her sides, her heart hammering in rhythm with the tension building inside her. She had tried to run from this moment, from this confrontation with herself, but now, before the broken mirror, she couldn't anymore.

Mirror shards looked back at her; each one told pieces she had not dared to face before. There is the cowering girl she once was, frightened and alone in a world she felt lost, watching as the Choir took her brother, Kaleb; and there is the warrior she was becoming-the one to fight silently inside to make sense of the silence that had both protected and trapped her. And then there was the version of her she did not yet know-the leader she had to be, the Silent who could harness the very thing she'd feared for so long.

Layla's hand stretched out, almost touching the glass which had reflected jagged, cold images, now alive with reflection. For a moment the reflection wavered as, for the first time, Layla looked. The fear that had been there, held like the silence, wasn't just of the Choir or what they'd done to her brother. It was a fear of herself-of the power she locked inside and was too afraid to use.

Her silence was once a cage-a defence mechanism in which to hide-behind, only to survive. There, standing there, Layla realized something she had never known before. Silence wasn't just the absence of words, though it could be something so much bigger than a shield. Layla's silence was hard-it was a strength-and she was only just starting to understand it. It was not submission. It was a choice.

She breathed deep, closing her eyes as the weight of her realization settled there. For so long, fear had ruled; but now, sitting in this room with parts of her broken and rearranged, Layla finally understood she didn't have anything to fear about it. The silence that was once a weapon for protecting herself from the world could now be a weapon used well and purposefully.

And stepping away from the mirror, Layla felt that silence around her shift. No longer confining or choking - now it was alive, almost. And then in the stillness, this voice rose. Not loud. Not out of the windows, or the bedroom door, or even outside, far out, but a voice from within, deep and calm and steady-sounding, much like the silence she'd finally begun to accept.

"I am more than my fear," the voice said.

Layla froze, her breath sticking in her throat. She'd heard voices before - the voices of doubt and pain, of guilt - but this one was different. It wasn't born of weakness. This was power, something she hadn't known she'd had inside her all along. The silence around her no longer felt like nothing. It was full, rich with the potential she'd always been too afraid to touch.

She continued walking towards the center of the room, slow, measured steps. The silence followed her, wrapping itself like a cloak, comforting and strong. The voice inside her grew louder with every passing second, not in volume but in presence. It was not the silence she was opposing. It was her ally and her strength. Layla had always been told she was weak: that she did not have power, that she did not have strength. Now lay eyes on reality: silence could be anything she wanted it to be. It could be strength. It could be power. It could be hers.

She was hit with the memory of Kaleb, one wave of ice in its suddenness. Layla hadn't thought of that day in too long, but now, it came back to haunt her with brutal clarity.

The sterile, white room. The Choir, standing over him like shadows, promising salvation. Promising peace. Layla had stood there, helpless, watching as they took him, erased him. Kaleb's vacant stare was burned into her mind, the final image of him she had before the Choir took his identity, his will.

She had blamed herself for all this time. Too feeble to stop them, too petrified to fight back. That helplessness haunted her; now, she's being pursued by a dark cloud, feeding into the silence she used to hide herself away from the world.

Her fists were clenched, and she could feel every fibre of her body tauten. However, this time, instead of yielding to the memory, there began something new within her: anger— or at least, cold, focused anger, rather than the chaotic disorganisation in her chest. The lies of the Choir she no longer cared for. The ache of having lost Kaleb, of failing him, no longer crushed her. She fed both of these flames.

The Choir had known silence to be surrender. But the days Layla was living, she learned that silence was not surrender. It was a tool, a weapon that could be made against them. She could watch. She could listen. And when the time was ripe, she could strike.

That evening, Layla was lucky enough to find Theo slumped over the cluttered table he always occupied, seated in deep contemplation regarding their next move. She hesitated for only a moment before approaching him, her steps measured, her heart steady. The silence had served her well, but now it was time to break it-not because she needed to, but because she chose to.

"I've been thinking," Layla said, her voice low but firm. "About what it means to be Silent."

Theo looked up, surprise dancing in his eyes at her forthrightness. He set the papers down he was holding and gave her his full attention.

Layla took a breath and then continued, saying, "The Choir wants to take all our identity away. They think they can silence us and take who we are. But what if we use that silence as a definition of who we are? What if we turn it into something they cannot control?

Theo blinked but didn't flinch. He sat calmly, but Layla saw a flicker of recognition in his eyes. He understood. Her words rang out with musicality, piercing him, despite the fact that he never said them. It was her hour, and Theo was sitting there to witness it.

She did not fear her thoughts for the very first time. She did not fear silence, for in doing so, she did not fear herself.

Scarcely had one mission ended when another was born, and Layla found herself among the Silents this time, her newfound resolve tested in the field. Tension coiled thickly, but as she took them through the dark corridors of the Choir compound, the stillness wrapped around her like armor, her focus sharper than it had ever been.

There was not a moment's hesitation when Layla faced the Choir enforcers. With one swift, silent gesture, she signaled to split up and take them into an ambush. It was fast and efficient, and when it was over, Layla stood there unmoving, listening to the silence after it.

Not onerous at all. It was triumphant.

Standing before the rest of the Silents after the mission, Layla's presence was demanding without one word. Layla had proven herself to lead, and more than the success of the mission itself, the onlookers looked at her in respect, the awe around their eyes changed. Theo stood back and gave a small nod to approve, but it was Layla who owned the room.

She did not have to say a word. Her silence spoke for her. She had faced the truth of who she was: not only a survivor, not just some piece of this rebellion. She was Silent. Once something that had held her by its chains, it now set her free and became something in which she was strongest-that she could use to push off the Choir to themselves. It was a defiant declaration-a proof of strength within herself. It was as though the weight of leadership settled onto her shoulders as she raised her hand to close the meeting. It wasn't heavy. It felt okay.

Episode 14: Plan of Attack

The room was dimly lit, yet the air seemed to thicken with tension as Layla stood tall at the center of the map projectors that burned their holographic display before her. There, in the center, lay the heart of the choir: a web of connected links and paths, security barriers that bound together every thread of influence this organism had. Layla knew the weight of the room, the expectation as her allies, Silents, gathered around the map, their eyes flashing between her and the glowing projection on the screen.

"Here," she began, her voice low but steady, tracing her finger over the map. "This is where we make our move."

The central node wasn't just a building; it was a fortress. Armed drones stood watch along the perimeter, biometric scanners guarded every entrance, and elite enforcers moved quietly inside the compound. Not quite what made it so dangerous. No, it was its intention—where the Choir controlled their network, where they processed data, tracked dissent, and manipulated society's neural connections. But the point wasn't merely to stop them; it was to take this information to the world.

Layla's eyes narrowed as she sketched the main goals. "In through the west tunnel," she told a corps of ready sergeants, her finger tracing along a narrow route that circumvented most of the outer defensive perimeter. "There we divide into two teams. Team A goes straight in on the node control center. There is where their converging streams of data go. We get to their mainframe from there. Team B makes for a ruckus in the east wing. We draw their people off from us."

She looked up at Theo. There he stood across from her, his face etched with determination. Yet, behind his shining, clear eyes, for one moment only, there flickered something--doubt. He was going to say it, she could tell. She felt his worries even before he'd opened his mouth to lay them before her.

This plan depends on the accuracy, Layla continued. One mistake, and the Choir will know we're in. We can't risk to give them any advance warning until we're already at the node. Once we gain the use of their systems, we send the proof of what we've learned out into the world.

But there was a murmur of assent, and then Theo emerged from the shadows, his voice slicing into the silence. "And what about drones and biometric scanners? Enforcers of the Choir? We are talking about levels of security we might be walking into a trap here."

Theo's words hung in the air as an unspoken fear gripped the room. The others shifted restlessly, their magnitude of the mission weighing them down.

Layla didn't flinch from the look she met from Theo. "I know it's dangerous," she said calmly. "But I have weaknesses in their systems. They've gotten too dependent on their own tech, and they're too confident in their systems. We can exploit that."

She tapped a row of marks on the map, indicating the holes in the Choir surveillance. "These are blind spots," she said, her finger tapping at their locations. "Places where their system lags in real time monitoring. Timing this just right, we'll be able to slip through undetected. But only if we stick to the plan.

His jaw stiffened, but he did not argue. He knew Layla had weighed it all, the risks and balances of power and the careful harmonies of danger. But behind all of it, the tension between caution and boldness still veiled the air.

"And what if the Choir has foreseen this?" Theo pressed on. "What if they believe we're coming?"

"We'll make enough noise on the edges to disguise our true intentions," Layla shot back with calculation. "It is a risk, but it is all we have".

The room fell silent once more, the weight of the plan settling upon them. They knew what was at stake-this mission might turn everything on its ear, or it might be their downfall.

Layla took a deep breath and paused. "There is one more thing," she said, her tone shifting. "The Silent Code".

At the mention of the code, some of the Silents exchanged skeptical glances. "You're talking about the encryption your brother told you about?" Theo asked, his brow furrowed, his voice cautious. "Layla, that information—

"I know," she cut across him, her eyes flashing with a mix of emotion and resolve. "I know it's dangerous. But it is our only chance to take out the Choir surveillance systems long enough for us to get in. Without it, we won't even make it past perimeter."

The room was silent. Layla could feel the unspoken questions hanging in the air. She hadn't said much about her brother, Kaleb, not since he was taken by the Choir. But now, his memory was tied into their mission, to their possibility of success. And she could sense their hesitation, their unspoken questioning if she could trust this code – if she could even trust herself.

Kaleb gave me the Silent Code before they took him," Layla said softly, her voice tinged with sadness. "He told me it was the Choir's greatest weakness. I believe in it and I believe in him,

She was silent, the implications settling. Layla didn't move, but she felt solid in her resolve. This Silent Code was not something to use for one's advantage, but a lifeline, the final thread of her brother without taint of the Choir. She would believe in it, though no one else did.

Theo moved forward again, his concern etched upon his face by something more than doubt—concern. "Layla," he started in a hushed tone, "I trust your judgment, but we need a contingency. What if it fails? What if we get caught?"

Layla looked at him for a moment, seeing the fear that was hidden beneath his expression. He wasn't worried about the plan; he was worried about her.

"'We need everyone in on this, Theo,' Layla said, her voice gentle but with a undertone of strength 'If we begin splitting up now, then we weaken our chances. We stick together.'

Theo let his eyes dwell there for a moment, searching hers, then nodded slowly. 'All right,' he said. 'We all go in together.

A silence settled over them, quiet and resolute. They all knew this could be their final mission, but now was no time to turn back.

Hours passed and Layla took the Silents through their final training. They moved silent ghostly presences through a simulated version of the Choir compound. They used hand signals and silent communication instead of voices. Every movement had to be perfect. Layla walked among them correcting stances, refining tactics, the silence no longer oppressive, but focused and intent.

When the training was finally over, Layla mustered her team to gather their small belongings, her eyes combing across each face. She didn't need to say much; in the silence they kept, a fire about determination was written.

"Tomorrow everything changes," she whispered softly into the air, as if her voice was enough to carry all that was left to be borne.

As night closed in, Layla stood alone on the rooftop, staring out at the skyline over the dark city. She could feel the crisp breeze and weigh the task settled on her shoulders. Footsteps came behind her and knew who it was before he uttered the first word.

Theo stepped up beside her, his grounding presence what she needed to focus on the present. "You ready for this?" he asked softly.

Layla didn't answer. She stared out through the lights of the city, miles away into darkness and possibility, and wondered how many lives would change by morning. "I don't know if anybody ever is ready," she said finally. "But we have to try".

Theo nodded, his hand pressing softly against her shoulder. "We'll get through this," he said steadily. "You've given us hope, Layla. That's stronger than all that the Choir has."

In the stillness that followed, they made an unspoken bargain in the dark. Whatever occurred, they would not give up. Together, they would see this end.

Tomorrow, the Choir would fall-or they would.

Episode 15: Crucial Role

The faintly glowing terminal cast its shadows across the skeletal walls of the hideout, moving upon the equally monochromatic face of Layla. The constant buzzing of the electronics filled the oppressive weightiness of the air. Layla gazed upon the scrolling stream of code on the screen before her. Her fingers hovered above the keyboard, unmoving, as the gravity of the task ahead of her began to settle within her chest like stone.

Paper, the job was straightforward: break into the Choir's mainframe and write in new core code. But for practice, it was a job only Layla could do. This would need the precision of a craftsman, the skill of an artist, and a mind sharp enough to understand and navigate the arcane structure of the most advanced system ever conceived. Only problem was she had only one chance. If she messed up—if her fingers hesitated, or her calculations were off by a fraction of a second— it wasn't just her life at stake. It was everyone in the resistance.

She closed her eyes slowly, exhaled long and slow, her mind churning the doubts. The weight of the responsibility threatened to crush her, and for the first time in a long while, she hesitated over her own abilities. Could she really pull this off? Could she fool something built to be unbreakable? The thought ate at her, refusing to let go.

No. Layla sat up in her chair. She wasn't doing this for her fears or her insecurities. She had to do it. She was the only one who could do it. They were all counting on her. The resistance was counting on her. This mission was their last hope to weaken the Choir's stranglehold on the world so there was a fighting chance at freedom. She had to push her self-doubts aside, at least for now.

A gentle knock on the door broke into her whirling thoughts; she made out Theo as he came in and was immediately met by his serious yet calm face. He always knew how to read her, even when she tried not to let him.

"Hey, okay?" Theo asked, placing a hand on her shoulder. His voice was soothing, grounding.

Layla imposed a forced smile. "Yeah, just. going over the plan.".

Theo didn't believe it, for one instant, but he didn't push. He nodded toward the terminal instead. "How about we run a few more simulations before we go live? We've got time."

Layla hesitated then nodded. "Yeah, that's a good idea".

She and Theo stood in the war room; she had set up a mock interface of the Choir's mainframe for training purposes. It wasn't an exact replica of anything, ever was, but it would do in a pinch to give Layla the practice she needed. Theo drew up beside her as she settled in front of the terminal, fingers flying across the keyboard to initiate the first simulation.

Everything went very smoothly for those initial minutes. Layla adeptly traveled her way through multiple firewalls and other security systems as if she were practicing on autopilot. But when the simulation got really underway, so did the challenge. Encryption layers started slowing her down after some time; then, without warning, an alarm-cue from the system that this was a detected intrusion.

Layla muttered a curse word under her breath. Furious, she pounded her fist on the desk before glaring at the red flash of error that splashed across the computer screen.

"It's just a simulation," Theo reminded her calmly, moving closer. "You'll get it."

Layla sighed, rubbing her temples. "I know. I just. I can't afford to mess up when it's the real thing. We don't get a second chance.

Theo sat beside her, his eyes skewing directly at hers. "Mistakes now are lessons for later," he said, incredibly light. "That's why we're doing this, right? So you'll be ready when it counts.".

His words wrapped around her like some sort of balm. It eased a part in her chest that had grown tight. Layla nodded, to herself, rather than to Theo. She needed to believe in that. She needed to trust every failure now counted as one step closer to success when it would be needed.

After running a few more drills, Layla went out for fresh air to clear her mind. Cool night air nipped at the skin of her arms as she wrapped them around her body. She looked at the stars dim through the brash lights of the city.

All of it hit her anew: the mission, the weight, the fear. There had once been a time not so long ago that Layla was responsible for no one but herself. When all she had to worry about was getting by each day, surviving under the rule of the Choir. Everything now is different. She is no longer just surviving. She is fighting for something greater.

But the pressure was crushing. What if she wasn't good enough? What if the others had made some kind of mistake, blindly entrusting her with their work? What if, when it counted, she flaked?

"You can talk to me about this," Theo's voice pierced through her ruminations. He had come outside after her, knowing she needed space but not wanting her to spin out without him.

Layla turned to him, doubt still weighing in her eyes. "I'm scared, Theo. What if I'm not strong enough? What if I do it badly?"

"You can," Theo said without hesitation. "You've already come this far, Layla. You're stronger than you think.".

She wanted to believe him. She really did. But the fear lingered, unwilling fully to let go. But Theo's words comforted her momentarily. They stood there together, shoulder to shoulder, with the weight of the next mission hanging between them.

The hideout was abuzz with excitement the following morning when Layla, among other important members of the resistance, appeared for the final briefing. Layla stood at the front of the hall, her voice poised as she attempted to explain the intricacies of the plan.

We'll have only one small window to break into the mainframe, she said, pointing at the holographic screen of the Choir's main system. "Firewalls in layers, encrypted. We have to go fast. The longer we take, the tighter security will be on our signal-and we'll have missed our window." Theo, out in back, spoke up. "What if something goes wrong?

She hesitated, reconsidering all possible scenarios. "If I can't rewrite the code in time, the Choir will adapt. They'll clamp down their control that much tighter, making any future attempts nigh on impossible. This. this is our best shot."

The room fell silent and quiet as the weight of her words settled over the group. Everyone understood what was at stake.

The others were departing for mission preparation; Layla retreated to her private quarters. She pulls out a small, weathered data drive from her bag—a gift from her brother, Kaleb. All she has left of him now. In it lies all the work he did on the network of the Choir-work that had landed him in a cell.

Layla stared at the drive, her fingers a little shaky as she plugged it into her terminal. Kaleb's code filled the screen in an intricate, beautiful mess of lines, flawless even. The better coder, more skilled and far less fearful, Layla wondered whether she was really good enough to finish the thing he had started.

But she had to try. This wasn't just about proving herself-it was about honoring Kaleb's memory, about freeing the world from the Choir's grip.

The countdown had begun on the mission.

Layla sat in tense silence in the transport vehicle, the engine roaring around them, filling the cramped space. Theo sat beside her, his presence steady, but even he couldn't dispel the growing knot of anxiety in Layla's stomach.

Layla gripped her gear tightly as they approached the mainframe of the Choir. Cramped and stuffed into its walls, there would be no room for hesitation once they broke through the walls. Every second would count.

Theo's eyes met hers. He subtly nodded his head. Layla took a breath, leveling herself out.

She was ready-or at least, she had to be.

SECTION BREAK: 2nd Pinch Point

A low thrum, it seemed, to match Layla's heartbeat, the hum of the transport vehicle reverberating softly through the metal floor. In the dim light she worked slowly, practicing efficiency, checking her equipment over and over again. Her respiration was smooth, controlled. There was no room for error because she had to be in control. Theo was rigid, staring across from her with a masked face. Layla could feel his presence steadying her, could feel his deadly determination leaching through the anxiousness in the air.

A mix of nerves, concentration, mixed together in the vehicle with the rest of the team. Out of the city, the alleyways and crumbling buildings were a blur of shadowed alleys and forgotten underbelly The Choir rarely ventured to, though they always kept an eye on. Beneath the city's surface, this used to be their temporary sanctuary until tonight, sanctuary was a fleeting illusion.

Layla regulated the tiny piece of machinery attached to her forearm, her mind rehearsing this mission plan over and over again, on the lookout for any flaw which might lead to something going wrong. Realizing their destination would lead to a critical node in The Choir's control network, a place which, if attacked, would start a wave of chaos through their enemy's communications. They had an opportunity to deliver a blow, to punch their wounds into the man and gain a little time, but they were running out of time.

Silence was punctured by Theo's voice. "We'll be there in five."

She nodded not trusting her voice just yet. Her stomach twisted tighter but outward she stayed cool. The eyes on her team bore down on her and the weight of the mission weighed on her. She didn't have the luxury of doubt.

Suddenly looking at Theo, she caught his eye for the briefest of moments. His steady gaze was enough. Weren't they through worse already? That gnawed away at her, though, and she couldn't get it out of her head. It felt too easy, too quiet. The instincts forged over the years of fighting gripped her and told her to stay alert. They'd never been this careless.

For the time being, it was working out just fine, and they were almost on their target. Layla breathed and forced the doubt to the back of her mind. We couldn't turn back now.

Its engine sputtered, and cutting off, the vehicle came to a stop. She led the team out, her boots smacking the cracking pavement of the alleyway with a soft thud. The night was very still and very dark. Not a breeze, no sounds of activity from above.

Theo moved over to her, perked his head slightly, listening, for anything out of place. The rag began to race through Layla's heart at the prickles in her senses. Too close to their objective, still. Her weapon tightened in her fingers.

They began to make their way further into the alley, the looming buildings on the sides throwing long expansive shadows. By the time the first shot cracked, Layla was going to send the team into position.

When the alleyway exploded into chaos before she even had time to realize what happened.

As the shadows turned to freight, the bullets began appearing out of them, muzzles lighting up the darkness like jagged lightning. Layla's heart pounded, and her instincts went against her and she dove for cover behind rusted dumpster. It had all been perfect; the ambush timed well. They knew. They knew they were coming, the Choir.

"Fall back!" Even Theo's sharp, commanding voice cut through the noise, but he sounded strained.

Layla peered out from behind cover, gasped at her breath caught in her throat. The enforcers were shades, their black tactical gear seeming to blend right in to the night, advancing with a cold rushing through her as they did. She returned fire as fast as she could, but before she could turn she was forced to run back behind the dumpster as a hail of bullets rained down on her.

She saw two of her teammates already down, their bodies lay motionless in the alley way. The madam clenched her jaw as she ran her mind over what their options were. Their ambush was airtight, the enforcers everywhere. No clear escape.

Theo's hand on her shoulder pulled her back further into the shadows. "You don't need to talk, just move!" he shouted over the gunfire.

Layla looked around. The only escape was there, ahead—a huge old industrial complex of rusting pipes and towering machinery. She let everyone know, without hesitation, that the rest of the team had to stay. She called: "Follow mew! Her voice was barely heard among all the chaos."

They ran.

Bullets passed them in a deadly symphony, ricocheting off the walls. Theo and Layla began sprinting away on the legs which were burning from the effort to get to the narrow passage that led to the complex. They faded the sounds of battle slightly as they crossed what threshold there was into the maze of metal and rust and the darkness of the towering pipes swallowing them.

The safety was only temporary though. She knew that they were being hunted.

The atmosphere changed inside the industrial complex. The gunfire was over, but she could hear the rhythmic whir of the Staff, the Choir's enforcers sweeping the complex. She was afraid of every creak of metal, every gust of wind in the pipes.

She breathed quietly and short, laying her breath behind a rusty machine. Theo wiped sweat from his brow, his jaw clenched, beside her. The others compressed themselves against the walls of the iron room, their faces haggard with fear.

Layla scrounged up a little terminal from her pack, mutated security system or not, she desperately wanted to access the complex's old security system. She was figuring out ways to lock a few doors, come up with a diversion, slow down their pursuers. The signal was weak and the screen in the terminal flickered in and out of static. Her forehead started sweating cold. In frustration she slammed her fist down on the terminal.

I glanced at her, seeing his expression grim. "He whispered, 'they're getting closer'."

The steady unrelenting footsteps of the Choir's enforcers underscored in Layla's ears with each passing second. Time was running out.

One of the remaining team members, Dorian, stood up as the enforcers closed in. He was grim determined.

'I'll draw them away,' he said quietly, without any quaver in his voice.

Layla's heart dropped. "Dorian, no—"

Before she could stop him Dorian ran from behind the cover, his footsteps echoing up the cavernous complex. His enforcers snapped to attention, and opened fire, following him in the opposite direction as their bullets chased him.

The silence was stifling, and the sounds of pursuit faded towards the distance.

Layla clenched her fists, her chest tightening with a bit of relief and guilt. At what cost did Dorian have bought them time? Theo nodded solemnly, she looked over at him. They couldn't stay here.

She whispered, barely above a breath, 'We have to move.' Theo nodded again.

The pair took off deeper into the complex and toward the far side, where an old sewer line ran beneath the city.

As they descended into the darkness of the sewer, the walls seemed to close in around Layla. She could feel the weight of the mission pressing down on her, heavier now than ever. They had lost so much, and yet, the fight wasn't over.

Not yet.

Episode 16: Direct Conflict

Long shadows went from the crumbling walls of the abandoned warehouse to the moon, which hung low in the sky. Layla was standing at the head of the Silents, inside, eyes scanning the smirks of her team. Their makeshift lanterns flickered, their weird patterns flickering across the rusted metal and concrete floors. Each Silent was preparing for the upcoming battle, there was a thick tension in the air, one before the storm.

She took a deep breath, slow and controlled, trying to calm her nerves. This was what she had been waiting for. The knot in her stomach just got tighter and tighter with each passing second, reminding her that now she would be the one responsible. It wasn't about survival at all. It was about proving herself, proving to the Silents, proving to herself. It took so long to be a part of something bigger and now that weight pushed down on her shoulders.

Her eyes moved across the room. Theo, as he was, had always been a calming presence; he nodding in her direction when he met her gaze. His quiet force of confidence in her was the one thing he could point to that at times pushed her through moments of doubt. Mira's face painted with determination and trepidation adjusted the strap of her weapon beside him. These were her people, her family in this war against The Choir. She turned and I closed my eyes as she looked back to the door, steeling herself.

Layla spoke firmly, "We stick to the plan." "We hit hard, we move fast, we don't stop once we've got our stronghold taken." No one fights alone. Or not at all, we do this together," said.

Their eyes sharpened with focus as the Silents gave murmurs of agreement. Now there was no room for hesitation. The door swung open and a slap of cold night air hit her in the face. It was time.

His throne was empty too, the streets outside just too quiet. In front of the Choir's, Silents moved in formation, staying safe in the shadows as they walked. Every muscle underneath Layla's skin taut as a bowstring, her eyes forward, waiting for the first gush of movement. Whilst they been training for weeks honing their skills, nothing could eliminate the gnawing fear in the pit of her stomach.

The Choir's enforcers appeared then, like clockwork, from the darkness. The heavily armored bodies passed into view as Layla saw them before their faces engulfed by cold, unfeeling masks. Layla could feel the familiar rush of adrenaline making her veins fill with adrenaline as they moved in deadly precision.

She raised her hand without hesitation and blew the signal. The Silents began to move. Rivers of gunfire had run through the streets, the cracks of bullets mixing with the pangs of metal and the screams of war. Her body went forward before her mind could figure it out, and Layla darted forward. The moonlight caught their blade, and an enforcer charged her. The enforcer poked forward with the weapon and whistled past Layla's ear just as she ducked, counter striking hard with a blow to the enforcer's ribs.

Her own impact reverberated up her arm, but she didn't hesitate. The enforcer in front of her spun and her blade found its mark; he crumpled to the ground. Another came at her too fast for Layla to throw a breath. Layla was unprepared for the sheer force of their first wave, it was relentless. These weren't your average soldiers, and they fought like every move was plotted to overpower.

Silents fought fiercely in the battle, excepting one. Her muscles burned, but she couldn't stop. Not now. Layla saw Mira, struggling against a wall on a gigantic enforcer whom she could not get away from. Layla charged, without thinking. Dodging gunfire and the deadly arcs of blades, she managed to weave her way through the chaos. Just in time, Layla struck him with all her strength, knocking him off balance right as the enforcer went for the killing blow. She forced the enforcer to the ground with a quick brutal slice.

"Stay focused!" Mira was pulled to her feet, she screamed and grabbed Layla by the arm. "We don't fall today!"

The noise faded but her voice cut through, and the silents rallied. They regrouped and pushed, renewed. The Silents were a wall, absolute, unbreakable, united, now the enforcers fought back with unrelenting force. The collective will grew with each step forward, she could feel the shift of the tide of battle.

When the chaos happened all around, Layla saw an enforcer from The Choir's elitist alongside. Her opponent stood over her in black armor, moving with an icy, graceless, coldly deadly grace. Layla's heart skipped a beat. A fear touched her for a split second, cause of past failures returning to her memory.

His weapon sliced through the air with brutal force and lunged. Layla's body reacted, dodging. The enforcer was fast — too fast — and she hadn't seen it coming. Her strength and each blow a test of her strength, each strike was met with a parry. Every dodge, every counter to Layla's fear melted away, replaced with something stronger; determination.

And this wasn't a fight for survival. The truth was she wanted to prove to Dan she had changed, she was stronger now. Her blade hit the enforcer over and over again, and every time she felt it, the growth, the power that had built up inside her since she became part of the Silents. But she wasn't that same scared girl anymore. She was a warrior.

Layla took advantage of the enforcer faltering for a moment and blinked in alarm. Precision strikes, her blade easily finding a hole in the enforcer's armor. Layla brought him to fall with a final, powerful beat, and he staggered.

The tide was turning. Layla and Theo were synchronized in how they moved and would attack relentlessly, alongside each other. Their determination spurred them every step, the Silents pressed forward. It seemed possible for a brief moment to reach victory. The stronghold was drawing closer and the enforcers were falling back. Layla was the first to feel it, before she saw it; a sense that something was shifting, looming.

"They're regrouping!" Her voice cut through the noise: Layla shouted. "Prepare for another wave!"

Soon after there came more; a wave of enforcers who stood taller and brought heavier weapons with them. Desperate battle ensued, the Silents trying to keep their position. Layla barked orders to keep her team together, rushing her mind. The enforcers were getting them, Layla knew, very close to being overwhelmed.

Layla suddenly realized that she is alone in the battle; at least she cannot see Theo and the rest of the group. She was totally outnumbered and her body was in severe pain with each step that she was taking. But she couldn't stop. Not now. Layla tried to push Rigoletto away with all the remaining power she had and her punches were becoming vengeful. It went down to a struggle between her and one soldier; then another soldier, her vision was blurred from tiredness but her determination was still strong.

Finally, after what seemed to Layla far too long, she was able to get past the line of enforcers and embraced Theo and all the other Silents. Both of them contributed their efforts to one last effort to succeed. The enforcers staggered back from their fierce onslaught and gradually the retreat began.

When the last enforcer touching the ground, a Layla existed among the burnt and destroyed vehicles, her breath ragged. The Silents had triumphed but they had done it at a great cost. The remnants of the battle, visible and otherwise, remained carved on the soldiers' faces; and that was just the start. But for now they were alive.

And Layla had shown it to her and her team, especially herself, that she would not fail her team by leading them through the dark.

Episode 17: Surprise Failure

The dust had not even had an opportunity to gather around their feet the faint echoes of the firing still ringing in the air but for more than a day there was silence. Layla had come to a complete stop at the edge of the destroyed structure the night air slowly filling her lungs as her eyes surveyed the vast empty land ahead. The Silents had barely avoided the latest wave of attacks and the win – if one could call it a win at all – was narrowly won. There were fewer now, many familiar faces gone, but they soldiers were still alive.

Theo came towards her, The passion in his eyes was no longer bright but still burning. He leaned against the wall beside her, out of breath, still for the moment, without even the energy to speak. Layla looked at him, studying the weariness that settled in every line in his face. It mirrored her own. The others, Mira, Jax and some other survivors joined them. Some patrolled clearing their guns, others sat or lay on the grill, bowing their heads a little as they enjoyed the little break.

I did… then a thought struck her that she felt something for years she had not felt… pride. It wasn't for her, no, not after she had disgraced herself more times than she cared to count but for them. In honour of Theo, Mira, Jax and all the other Silents who have struggled to draw their last breaths. They had traveled so far, they had fought the enemies of fate and death, and now they simply went on fighting. Their eyes met for a second and Layla saw it in Theo's eyes, they did not have to talk, they both would comprehend what the other had gone through.

"We're still here," Theo spoke softly, after a long moment.

"Yeah," Layla replied, her throat tight. "We are."

But before she could say it, a worm of doubt began twisting in her stomach, more insistent than anything he had said to her in days. The calm, it seemed to me, was too frail, too soon vanishing. She understand more than anyone how dangerous things could be, but now, she thought that there was a possibility for her and the child. Perhaps, a die-hard hope, it was successful at their end too. Perhaps they had at last defeated The Choir. It absurd, yet a thought that was warranting Layla's fate, she could not help but allow it to seep in.

The strike of metal against metal interrupted the calm:

Layla turned to the sound quickly and her heart began racing. In the recording it started from outside, close to the entrance of the alleyway. Then in rapid successions, one could hear the deadly sounds of gunning sounds very clearly.

"Get down!" Layla screamed as loud as she could for fight or flight had officially kicked in.

The Silents scattered. Sam clutched Layla's hand tightly and she dragged Theo down the moment the bullets flew and impacted on the walls. Fear arose and the previously orderly withdrawal turned into a complete mess, and The Choir's goons invaded the construction site with deadly efficiency. Layla felt her heart beat steadily and, helplessly her brain tried to grasp the reality of matters. How? How had they known?

"The Choir's been waiting for us," Theo grated, reaching for his gun and firing back.

Layla's stomach dropped. They had been outmaneuvered. The air around her filled with the sound of gunfire she barked orders her throat hurting as she tried to make herself heard. "We need to fall back! Get to the west exit!"

But it was too late. The enforcers were all masked and clad in some armor that made them move like true machines, devoid of emotion. Layla replied and the enemy surrounded them, thus blocking the roads used to make their escape. She felt the familiar knot of fear in her heart – the dreadful emptiness of failure.

"Layla!" Theo's voice brought her back from her reverie but when she opened her eyes she saw that he was fighting one of the spider like enforcers. Layla tried to get closer to him but stopped when more of The Choir's soldiers emerged in the way. She fought her way through, slashing and dodging, but with every step, the distance between her and Theo seemed to stretch further.

Mira was the next one who fell down, pulled on the floor by two enforcers. Jax had been outsmarted and handcuffed within a blink of an eye,, struggle was futile. Layla gulped down a breath as she watched him let them fall one by one. Her companions, her kin, everybody being captured right before her.

"No!" Layla shrieked, her vocal folds raw as they passed through air to slash at the enforcer next to her. Finally she scored on one of them but there was always another one coming. Layla turned to kick him again and crashed into the side of the car, a pain piercing her ribs – she was hit again in the back and found herself on the floor her head spinning.

Suddenly, hands clawed into her wrists and twisted them around her back. Layla tried to stop it, shook her head fiercely and tried to free herself but the grip got only stronger. She found a moment to free her right hand and punch one of the enforcers on the face but before she could do anything else, she was brought down again by another punch on the head.

Most of the time her vision became impaired and the periphery of the world was fading away. I described Layla – broken in body and spirit – simply lying down in the bed. The feeling of failing her lover broke her chest as if a huge load was placed on it.

She had failed them. They had received her leadership by following her in the direct trap and now… all of them they were going to suffer for that.

Even the enforcers from before betrayed no emotion as they herded the Silents like cattle. Layla knew something cold and metallic closed around her wrists, and the feel of the chain around her neck. Again, she was pulled to her feet and all her muscles screamed in objection at the treatment as she was pulled into another section of the building, which appeared to have been converted to a temporary jail. It was cramped; the mood was almost palpable and smelled of blood and lost battles.

She sit on the wall defeated, her hair hanging below her nape, her face pale, her head thumping, hands tied. Beside her, chained was Theo who looked bruised and beaten but well alive. Mira and Jax had also arrived; they would not make eye contact and both had lost all semblance of hope. Layla clenched her heart when she saw them. How had it come to this? How in special ways had she failed them all?

She started wondering with every choice she had made wrong, every mistake they had made that got them here. She had been sure of the plan, sure that they could escape The Choir and build themselves a new life. But now, instead of hope, hatred and anger, she only saw the despair wrenched on the faces of her comrades. She had failed them and the feeling was audible, as if the oppressive feeling of despair cloaked her completely.

Layla closed her eyes, she attempted to remove the guilt, the shame from her mind but it followed her everywhere. Regret had become a storm in her mind, which was even more intense than any one of the regrets that filled her head. Perhaps she was not the commander they required. Or maybe she was never meant to be with me.

But then, something shifted. Suddenly wide awake, something caught the attention of Layla eyes and she quickly sat up from her covers. The enforcers went about their work with clueless determination and their movements were almost robotic and so carefully planned. It was very slight but it was enough to make Layla have this little thought in her head.

She quickly looked at Theo from across the room and signaled at him to follow her. He glanced at the man, unbelieving for a moment, then it came back to him. He also saw it now: something was amiss.

Maybe… maybe all wasn't lost.

And suddenly, in the deepest blackness, there was a tiny pinch of light.

Episode 18: Siren Song of Hope

It was thick in the air of the hideout—blood and sweat and fear left hanging, stuck inside the little cave. Layla heard the others speaking softly, their voices heavy with exhaustion and numb clarity that came only from almost not being there anymore. She knelt beside Theo, her hand shaking as she pressed a cloth to the side where he'd taken the deep cut of the fight.

Theo winced but said nothing, his eyes scanning the room, looking everywhere but at her. He didn't need to say it; they both knew how close they'd come to losing everything.

"They weren't human," Layla muttered, breaking the silence between them.

Theo's gaze snapped to hers. "What are you talking about?"

Layla drew back the cloth, and pressed it harder, allowing the warmth of the blood to seep through to his skin. She was trying to keep her mind sharp, trying not to let that nagging thought in the back of her head creep in, but she couldn't help it. "The enforcers. You didn't see it? Their eyes, Theo. Like there was nothing there. No fear, no anger-just nothing.".

Theo grunted as he shifted, pushing himself up on his elbows. Clenching his jaw, fighting the pain, but a hardness was there in his expression to match the look he gave her. "You are just tired. We all are. They're trained for this. The Choir programs them like soldiers, conditioned not to feel."

That's not it," Layla insisted. Her voice was low, but there was an edge to it. She looked toward the corner of the room where they'd restrained one of the enforcers they'd caught. His body lay slumped against the wall, bound but eerily still. She could see his eyes—vacant, almost dead. "It's not conditioning, Theo. It's something else. They were like machines.

Theo shook his head, irritation creeping into his voice. "You're reading too much into this."

But Layla couldn't shake the feeling. She had felt it during the fight, and now, watching the enforcer barely react to being captured, it gnawed at her. Something was wrong. "I'm going to find out," she said, pushing herself up and making her way toward the enforcer.

She knelt beside him, her chest thumping with the heavy beats of her heart. He was too young for his eyes to be so blank. His face was too young. His eyes began searching for her within their own whiteness. "What is your name?" she asked herself to be able to say it with a calm voice, though all fibers of her body screamed out for answers.

The enforcer said not a word. His eyes blinked slowly, as if awakening from a long slumber. Layla asked again, this time louder. The words only came out of the enforcer's lips but were nearly a whisper.

"Where are you from?" Layla pushed, her frustration working its way through her. She needed him to talk, to give her something that would make clear what she already suspected.

Again, the enforcer blinked. His glance rose to meet hers, no recognition, no understanding. "I. I don't know," he whispered, his voice hollow.

Layla's breath caught in her throat. "You don't know where you're from?"

The enforcer shook his head, his eyes confused and looking lost. A child trapped in a nightmare, "I. can't remember."

Her stomach twisted. This was wrong—deeply wrong. She glanced back at Theo, who was watching her from across the room, his face set in stone. But the doubt in his eyes betrayed him. Even he couldn't deny that something was off now.

Layla turned back to the enforcer. "Who are you? Why are you with The Choir?"

Again, the enforcer's response was a broken jigsaw of words. "I. I don't know. I don't remember. It. hurts to think."

Layla's heart was racing with the fear of what was happening. That wasn't conditioning and training. That was much, much worse. "Theo," she whispered, her voice straining up into a whisper, but he could hear the fear. "I think they're being controlled—like their minds are being erased."

Theo's silence was deafening. He wouldn't hear of it, but truth lay there in black and white.

That night, Layla couldn't sleep. She couldn't erase the blank stare of the enforcer from her mind. She reclined in her bedroll on the cold concrete floor; however it wasn't the chill seeping in through the bones that kept her awake. Questions swirled about in her head that she couldn't answer. If The Choir possessed such power, what did that mean for their struggle? How could they ever hope to win if an enemy could even strip people of their minds?

At midnight, Layla made a decision. She couldn't wait. She had to know the truth.

It had once been a bustling outpost, now abandoned and quiet, except for the distant hum of the city and an occasional whip of wind through broken windows. Layla and Theo moved through the rubble with care, each step calculated, eyes scouring every shadow. They came here to find answers, and Layla was certain they would.

Inside, the chill light of a burst console flickered, casting weird shadows around the room. Layla's heart was pumping hard as she moved through to the machines. There were dangled wires from the ceiling, like veins; rows of headsets scattered on the floor; monitors all along the walls, flickering through scenes of the shattered brainwaves.

Theo moved closer his face tightening.

"What is this place?

Layla pushed down a hard swallow, acid rising in her throat. "It's where they control them. Look at these machines-they're built to erase memories, install thoughts. This is how The Choir makes people into completely mindless soldiers."

Theo clamped his hand around the back of a chair; his knuckles went white. "You're saying they're. slaves? That they chose this?"

Theo hammered his fist on the console, the crack of the sound fills the room. "We can't afford this," he muttered, squeezing out a rather irate whisper. "We can't begin treating them like victims. We need to win this war, Layla."

Layla's chest contracted. She comprehended his anger, but she could not ignore the truth. "But what if we are wrong, Theo? What if we are fighting people who don't even know they are in a war? How could we justify killing them?"

Theo clenched his jaw. "We don't have the luxury of thinking like that.".

There was such a heaviness in the silence between them- Layla felt that, and yet still she could not let go of the truth she had uncovered.

That night, back in the hideout, Layla stood alone on the rooftop, surveying the broken city ahead. The truth weighed heavy in her chest, a burden she didn't know how to carry. Her tears blurred her vision as she fully understood the horrors of their situation. The fight is no longer for freedom, but rather a fight for the minds of people they were meant to save.

Grief for the people they had lost, for the lives they had taken, washed over her like a tidal wave. She sank down to her knees sobbing quietly in the night. How could they ever hope to win when the enemy wasn't just The Choir, but the very system that controlled people's minds?

But dawn broke, and Layla stood again, her will weak but unbroken. She had made her decision. They weren't fighting to break The Choir anymore. They were fighting to break its hold on the enforcers.

"We're not fighting to win anymore," she said to Theo, her voice firm, even if not entirely certain in her own heart. "We're fighting to save them.".

SECTION BREAK: 2nd Plot Point

Explosions tear the night air apart, casting sharp, jerky flashes on the crumbling walls of the Silents' last haunt. The air reeks of ash and gunpowder, choking and noisome. Layla's heart thudded in her chest; her breathing ragged, she pushed forward into the fray. The attack had come fast, brutal, sooner than she had let herself believe. The dark combat gear made the Choir's enforcers faceless; they swarmed the hideout like some plague, methodical and merciless.

In her hand, Layla gripped a pistol slick with sweat, but it suddenly weighed heavier than it ever had before. Her meticulous plans-the ones she'd spent weeks agonizing over-were unraveling right in front of her eyes. She watched in horror as one member of the Silents after another collapsed to the ground, bodies crumpling into dust, some screams echoing through her mind as they begged for help. And she could not save them. Not this time.

The fire in her belly, which had seen her through so many battles, now seemed to flicker out, embers barely warm against such ruin. Explosions echoed and the sharp ping of gunfire through her numb shock. She could hear the dying crying out, see the terrorized look in the faces of the living. It was the first time in ages that Layla was frozen. The mind was racing, but the body unable to do even as much. How did it come to this?

She tripped on debris to try to find some way to process the mess, but every step dug deeper into the tight-fitting suffocation of failure. More explosions came now, closer, making the earth shudder beneath her. She could hear Theo screaming, see him yanking someone to safety, but his voice cut little clear of her deepening fog.

They were losing ground. Every second, The Choir was forcing her closer to the abyss of oblivion, and Layla had no answers. No strategies. Just the brutal reality of death and failure coming for her. A bullet whizzed off the wall next to her, snapping her back into the here and now. Layla ducked involuntarily, erratic heart pounding harder, fear clawing through her insides. She battled her way out of the hideout, just dodging the enforcers. But with every step she took, it weighed heavy with guilt—every life lost on her watch felt like a knife twisting deeper.

When Layla had moved closer to the edge of the safe zone, the grief and confusion in her mind became a blurred haze. The clash of battle continued to move further and further away from her, but the bitter taste of defeat lingered on. Layla had lost people before, but this-this was different. She'd led them into the disaster and now they were paying the price.

The Collapse of Trust

In the barren streets of this city, there they were—survivors from the Silents—holed up together, nervous glances being darted into every shadow, every faint sound that managed to grab their attention. The once strong group which had stood through The Choir now seemed broken and disheartened, the spirits hanging by a thread of a thin thread. Layla could feel their stares—that accusatory gaze which was filled with questions they did not need to ask.

Theo stood there, in the middle of the group. He had dirt and blood smeared across his face. His fists were bunched up at his sides as well. Camaraderie between him and Layla, long locked in an unspoken bond, now fractured into bitter silence that had never been between them. He had always been her most loyal ally, but tonight had seen that loyalty tested far too much.

What the hell happened, Layla?" Theo's voice cracked the silence like thunder. His calm eyes flared in anger. "How did they know? How did The Choir find us?

The question hung in the air, weighty and laden. Layla's throat choked up. She opened her mouth to answer, but the words refused to pass out of her lips. How would she explain? She had misjudged, trusted faulty information, failed to discern the next move that The Choir was going to make. The weight of it was crushing down upon her, but Theo was not done.

"They knew exactly where to hit us," he continued, stepping closer, his voice rising. "People are dead, Layla. Our people. Because of your decisions."

The rest of the group shifted uneasily, their faces betraying their own doubts, their own resentment. Layla's stomach churned, her mind racing for an explanation, an excuse, but none came. She had nothing to offer them but her guilt.

As if his statement did not convey enough, another voice chimed in. "You were supposed to keep us safe," Jared said, another newer recruit. His eyes were wide with fear, and his voice did not remain steady. "What's the point of fighting if we're just going to die like this?"

Theo looked up at the team, his face a mask of frustration and betrayal. "We're done here. This fight. it's suicide."

The murmuring in the group grew louder, higher-pitched, some nodding, others silent but for all intents and purposes: torn. The fracture ran deeper. Layla felt she stood at the edge of a crumbling cliff, watching everything she built crumble, piece by piece. The Silents had always trusted her. But now? They looked at her as though she were the enemy. And the worst part was that she couldn't blame them.

Haunted by Failure

Later that night, Layla snuck away from the rest of the group, her chest tightening with the emotion she could not quite place. She ran into an abandoned building on the outskirts of town, far enough along that she could leave all the others behind with her thoughts. The room was cold and dark, moonlight barely penetrating through cracked windows, but it did its work by casting dust everywhere, unestimated and forgotten—just like she felt.

Sitting on the ground, Layla tried to pull her knees to her chest in an attempt to contain her breathing. But before her eyes, ghostly and unshakeable images of the killed just flashed by. She closed her eyes tight, yet immediately all the terrible scenes of the ambush appeared: blood, fire, screaming and anguish of the helpless.

Layla ran her shaky hands through her hair, tugging at the strands. She had failed them all. She had led them all into a death trap, and here were the survivors, broken and directionless. Could she still be said to be a leader?

She turned her gaze to a broken mirror propped against the wall, shards of glass reflecting a bad picture of herself. Layla gazed at that reflection, gazed at the empty eyes that stared back. Was she the fierce, determined leader who had held firm against The Choir for so long, or the broken woman sitting here now, consumed by guilt and fear?

Layla's head began to spin through darker, darker spirals. So much had gone wrong, so many deaths inflicted. Maybe Theo was right. Maybe the time to stop was now.

The offer of surrender

The silence was like a weight upon her when a soft creaking of a door opening behind her made Layla freeze where she stood. Her hand instinctively went to the grip of her gun, though she didn't draw it. A figure entered the room behind her, moving quietly, deliberately. Layla's heart skipped a beat. An agent of The Choir.

Episode 19: Symphony of Struggle

She stood on the edge of what had once been their sanctuary, but now were ruins. There was almost suffocating silence around her, just a crutch of crackle of dying embers and the occasional creak as debris shifted in the wind. This was the once stronghold for the Silents, the people she had promised to protect, nothing more than a graveyard of walls broken, lives shattered.

Her eyes traveled over the wreckage but she didn't actually see it. Her eyes were glazed over and empty, like they were all the fire she ever held inside her was gone. First her lips trembled slightly, then her hands started to as well. It was going to work its way through her body, she clenched them into fists, willing the tremor to go away, but it wouldn't. The failure reminded her with every fallen stone, with every streak of blood on the ground.

Failure.

Her wound had gnawed at the word constantly. The hideout's physical destruction hardly hurt her but what it stood for did. It had been more than just a base. She had let it fall, a hope symbol, a haven for those who had nowhere else to be. Her leadership had been trusted. Her strength. Now the Silents were left with nothing but rubble as they had put their trust in her.

She couldn't fall, not yet, not here, her legs felt weak. It drove the weight of her own self loathing down on her chest like an iron vice. She reminisced on the people who had depended on her: the lives she couldn't have saved. Without realizing it she pictured each face as though it were a nightmare that she couldn't wake from. She knew it was her decision, her choices that had brought them here and she decided she couldn't take any more.

The screams, the explosions, the faint echoes of the ambush she could hear, though still. They had let the Choir come so easily and she had been powerless to stop them. The price of that was too much for Layla to bear, in the quiet aftermath of that, trying to do the right thing.

The poor girl, she stumbles back to her quarters, the one space she had always retreated to, when the world got too loud, too chaotic. It was a small room, lit dimly by but a single flickering bulb. The walls themselves were closing in on her, making it feel cold. As she closed the door and turned the lock behind her, she was doing it slow, deliberate, as though the action might somehow close out the tempest of thoughts ravaging her mind.

Layla was just standing there… her back to the door… breathing raggedly, unsteadily. The very thought of the noise in her head and around her kept playing itself over and over, circling about her brains as she made different attempts to silence them and give her a moment of rest. She wanted to scream, to rage at the world, at herself, but she had no energy to do anything more than that.

Her eyes fell onto the map, still pinned to the wall. The edges were crumpled and hastily scribbled plans and strategies marked it. The same map they'd used to plan their last mission. The mission that had resulted in disaster. In two quick strides Layla crossed the room and grabbed the map off the wall as she stared at it for a long painful moment. They had lived by it, had guided by it, now it was just a vestige of a failed life.

Layla crumpled the map in her palms and frowned, letting out a guttural sound so deep she could swear the sound came from her very insides, then threw the map towards the ceiling. A soft thud, it hit the wall and fell to the floor along with the other scattered remnants of her broken, yes broken plans. Her chest was rising and falling, tears were at the corners of her eyes. But she didn't cry. She refused to cry.

It seeped into layers she hadn't been aware existed, down dark passages she'd long forgotten existed, reshaping the terms of her self loathing. The Choir wasn't angry with her. No, this wasn't their fault. This was hers. She had made the calls that had cost lives and she had led them in here. Or perhaps she wasn't able to lead anymore. Maybe she never had been.

Instead, her body was heavy from exhaustion, but her mind would not stop. Layla sat staring at her ceiling, her fingers tapping at her thigh with each thought more ambitious than the last. Memory jumped to memory, the faces of those who died, the ambush. The explosions in the air, the terrified screaming of the Silents, and all of the lifeless bodies strewn across the ground flickered in and out of focus.

She drew her chest tight as she went over every moment again. There was nothing to do to escape it, there was nothing to do to turn it off. The guilt was suffocating. It pushed down on her and made her feel she couldn't breathe. She'd done everything she could to keep everyone together, to protect them, but everything was now broken. She stood alone, and in the silence she knew she was alone.

Everyone had turned away. The weight of what she hadn't done, what she hadn't chosen, what she could still have done. Sleep did not come, and Layla's eyes fluttered closed. Only the memories. The weight of her failure.

Her body was in agony and she forced herself to sit up. Layla could see her old journal on the small table that lay beside her cot in the dim light. The pages of it were creased and dog-eared from years of use, it was worn. It is the sort of letter you keep put away for years. She slowly reached for it, tracing the edges with her once familiar fingers that flipped it open.

Somewhere she had written the words and it stared back at her, foreign, like they didn't belong to her. Someone stronger. Layla stopped on an essay on a page where she'd written her promise to herself—to never give up. She could almost recall a dream version of herself that was just younger, more hopeful, but the memory was distant.

She got herself to read the words aloud and what happened when she got to the final line… Who was that person? The one who believed so strongly in their cause? She didn't even know who she was anymore. Her eyes burned as she held the journal to her chest shaking uncontrollably with her hands. How had she fallen so far?

She stood by the window watching the fires in the distance, stretching as far as the horizon stretching. They were out there, and they were the Choir's forces, ever reminding you there was a fight that never seemed to end. There was a cold light from the moon over the city and Layla allowed herself to imagine walking away for the first time. To surrender.

To let go of the burden, to stop fighting, to erase yourself from the responsibility of everyone's lives. It was terrifying and comforting. What if she just gave up? What if she let The Choir win? Would the world be any worse off without her?

Then, she gazes down at the little dagger laid on the table-a gift from one of the Silents. Symbol of trust and of alliance. Layla reaches out to claim it, holding the cold weight of it in her palm. The sharp edge catches the flickering light of the candle, and for an instant, Layla is frozen where she stands, suspended between two choices.

Was she thinking of throwing it out for good as a symbolic way of surrender or continued holding on owing to still many people's dependence on her?

Episode 20: Pep Talk

His footsteps in the wreckage of the hideout are barely audible, his eyes trailing to her as they take him in. Her body hunched in the corner, half immersed in shadows, Layla sits. A single candle flickering lightly on a cracked table; the light illuminates the walls in patterns from which no one overhead dreams of beauty.

The debris settling cracks, alone except for the occasional crack. Her face is hidden; her posture is broken. She's small now, beyond the light, in her own darkness. She feels its weight, thick air of her despair. By her hard fighting, she was once the Layla who has led them all in fervid resolve.

Softening his movements now he approaches, he takes a breath. The last thing he wants is to intrude on her grief, and he knows she càn't stay this way. Not now, not when so much is riding on it.

Sitting at the foot of her bed, he whispers, but what he says, who knows? "Layla..." It is a word with a weight thicker than that of itself. It's an invitation to speak, but also a lifeline, a quiet lifeline to the world she won't be able to stay in a moment.

There's no response at first. Layla's gaze doesn't waver from the candle's flame that flickers, unflickering, like a bit of flame in a wide silence. His heart tightens in his chest as The stares at him. He can see that, since the last battle, the weight that she no longer shoulders makes her shoulders sag under an invisible weight, the hollow exhaustion in her eyes.

Theo puts his hand on her shoulder gently and lets out a long pause, grounding her, or at least slowing her a little. She opens her lips, and still does not say anything. The silence bills across them, a thin string of a thing.

"Are you okay?" Theo's voice is gentle, but even he knows the answer before she can speak it.

Finally, Layla shifts, and she flicks her gaze toward Theo, but doesn't look at him. Her expression is defeat and weariness, as if it is too much to even begin answering him.

Theo doesn't push. He stays by her but waits. In moments like these, sometimes there isn't anything else to say than silence. The Layla he remembers isn't the young girl he fell in love with in the early days—the girl who knew exactly what to say and who always held the rebellion up on her back. It's not that Layla, and he does know.

It's what feels like an eternity, but Layla finally does speak, barely more than a whisper. "I failed them, Theo."

But Theo doesn't interrupt; his breath hitches. He waits.

"They trusted us... and we are looking like this." Her hand trembles slightly as she gestures weakly at the ruined space around them. I don't even know who I am anymore. I might not be the person they need. Maybe I never was."

These are raw, cutting words that are a confession. Theo notices how her fingers shake in her lap, how she doesn't look present, like she's gone somewhere half gone, somewhere she may never be back from.

Theo has a quiet, steady voice, yet filled with emotion when he says, 'You're wrong.'. His presence firm and unwavering. "You haven't stopped being the person they need." You've taken us into unendurable times. You've outdone us all. That doesn't all go away in one failure."

Tears appear in her eyes, she shakes her head. "I don't remember that." said that yesterday. Then I was different... stronger. Look where it got us."

Theo looks around, taking in the wreck, the toppling stones, the wreckage of what was their last safe place. She's lost in her own mind and he knows it. He can't let her stay there, but he does.

Theo responds with a rise in his voice but not with rage, but with passion: "It got us here." "We're still here. You're still here. And that means something."

Her brow furrows, and she turns to him. "Does it? Does it really matter? Perhaps it's time for me to turn over to another? I can't—"

"Stop." Theo's voice is firm now. He's down on his knees, right in front of her, leveling his head into hers. "You're not this one loss." Would any of us have survived this long without you? You've saved lives, Layla. Even when everything around us has been falling apart, you've kept hope alive.

He grabs the little dagger lying there, one Layla once used to represent leadership but now lies discarded. The blade catches the faint light and Theo holds it up. "This isn't just a weapon. It's a reminder. A reminder of everything you've done for us and everything we've fought for. You're still the one who carries it. You always have been."

They rest the look of their eyes on the dagger, their eyes soften. In the flicker of something she has, deep inside her, the memory, maybe, or there is such a tiny spark of belief that maybe she hasn't lost her completely. It seems her hands are trembling so they brush against the cool metal as she extends her hand to pull it out.

For a moment, she hesitates. Slowly, she puts her hand around the dagger's hilt, underneath the hide that it's sheathed in, feeling it's weight. Layla's emotions raw and exposed; the silence between them getting thicker as she can feel her breath catch in her throat.

Theo's heart is in his throat and he watches her closely. Behind her eyes he can see the battle: try as she may, her failure is crushing her again, weighing her down; she can't help but believe in herself again. "You're not done, Layla. There is so much you have left to give. Don't let this be the end."

Layla clutches the dagger so tightly around the hilt that her knuckles belong white. Her chest rises and falls with a long, shaky breath and she exhales. For a second what feels like she looks up at Theo, really into the eyes.

She doesn't have any fire in her gaze, not yet. But there's something else too—a small, determined lump that isn't quite gone, and never really was.

Theo is there to steady her after she rises to her feet but she's unstable for a moment. Layla grips the dagger tightly, feeling its weight, its purpose.

Equally terse, her voice is quiet but firm: 'You're right.' "I'm not done yet."

His relief is plain on his smile as she takes back the strength she thought was gone. They stand, together, amid the ruins, and for the first time since days the future doesn't look so grim.

Episode 21: Reclaiming the Sound

They left her in the remains of the safe house alone. What small light it was, tracking in through the cracks in the wall, the air thick with dust. She could see a shattered mirror hanging precariously from the wall, jagged shards hanging off, brushing past her face, reflecting her face in pieces. She eyed each piece of broken glass, which acted as a distorted replicas—a disjointed reflection of herself—each one. However it wasn't with fear, oh no the pounding was just her heart. It was something else. There was a quiet intensity to it.

Her eyes narrowed and focused to the largest shard of the mirror. The expression in determination was set on part of her face, and it reflected it. Her knuckles were white against the cracked wooden table, clenching her hands on the edge in front of her. Her past, the weight of it all — failures and losses, even doubt — was weighing on her but something had changed. She was running from being alone, scared of being alone, if she was alone she was afraid that no one would follow.

Layla had a thing about broken mirrors, and she stared as they all shattered except her own, except now she saw something she hadn't let herself see. The pieces weren't just broken fragments of who she was. They were what she had come to be. It was all part of the whole; they trial, they wounds, their victories. She was not incomplete. She was not weak. All the cracks in her reflection only made her stronger.

Her fingertips touched jagged edge, one shard. Sharp, but it was cold to the touch, and she didn't pull back. The pain was familiar. The reminder of everything she had survived. One slow, steady breath escaped her lips as her hand rested against the mirror just for a moment longer before she pulled away.

Come, she whispered, in silence. No more of her broken reflection felt like a reflection of her flaws but a reflection of her resilience. Fear of isolation had taken too long for her; true strength is being alone when the need presents itself, not because she had to, but because she wanted to.

Layla pulled away from the mirror and walked across to a secret compartment built into the floor. Each step was deliberate but her movements were grounded her her decision. She crouched, pried open the wooden panel and saw the secret she'd denied for so long. A faint shimmer of its hilt lay nestled in a bed of cloth, inside, making the sword long and ornate.

She gasped as memories played through her mind of when she used to reject this weapon, that only true leadership and connection would find in shared burden. She knew that connection wasn't the same as dependence. Isolation wasn't the same as autonomy. The choice to lead was leadership, the will to stand alone but accept no-one else into the fight.

Layla reached for what looked to be a sword, moving slow for a moment. She felt the weight of it hit her palm the moment her fingers wrapped around the hilt. The weight of responsibility wasn't anymore—it was the weight of control, of agency. The blade caught the light, as she lifted the sword. But her look changed from uncertainty to resolve. This was her moment. This was to be the decision through which everything that followed would eventually be judged.

There was nothing scary in remembering past battles. It was reminder, lessons of how much she had come. Those were fears that she didn't realize were behind her now, or behind her at all: fear of isolation, fear of being left behind, of being 'left out,' of being 'left behind.' Layla tightened her grip on the sword, the steel cool but comforting in her hand. The future lay ahead, and with it, the ultimate confrontation with the Choir.

Layla stood as she saw a little envelope tucked under the compartment where the sword kept hiding. Then she kneeled down to retrieve it. The edges of the paper were frayed as though it had been waiting for her all her life. Warily she opened it, and unfolded the letter inside. She knew this handwriting, it was a familiar one, a message from a fallen comrade, someone who believed in her, even when she didn't.

"Layla you always knew what should be done." "We even saw it when you couldn't see it yourself." Yet her praise was steady, her throat squeezed tight with emotion as she read the words aloud. The letter highlighted not only the sacrifices made, but faith others had placed in her. Her eyes filled with purpose, she folded the letter, slipping it into her pocket. It wasn't just for her — it was for everyone who bought into what they were fighting for, everyone who stood by her.

Once it no longer felt like the weight of leadership. It felt right.

Layla came out of the safehouse; she stepped out with the sword at her side into the cold air. Before her, in ruins: the lasts of the rebellion's darkest times, the bombed, the ruins of buildings that they had fought to protect, the faces of her friends that she had failed to save. The ghosts of her past failures passed by her on the hollow streets in the wind. But Layla didn't flinch.

As if to prove that purpose, she had walked through the wreckage, never faltering, never hesitating. Every shadow, every memory that used to haunt her was farther and farther away now, like a past self she had out of her. The faces that had passed before her eyes, the crumbled buildings were all they had endured, and she knew. She stopped in the center of the street, exhaling slowly. The fire in her eyes burned brighter than ever as she whispered to herself, "I'm not afraid anymore."

The wind whipped around her, but it no longer carried the weight of her fear.

Layla gathered her remaining allies later at the middle of the'made managed headquarter. Silent they stood before her, expectant. It was a sword in her hand, a symbol of what was to come. She scanned their faces; hardened, by battles fought, but given to the cause they believed in.

Layla started, 'We're about to deal with the Choir.' "And we will win. It's not about following me, I want you to understand that. It's about choosing to fight. No matter what that cost." Then she paused, allowing her slow words heave over the room.

Subtle nods of approval were what they were. They all made eye contact with Layla, solidifying not followers but equals. She brought the sword up and they all grabbed theirs, ready to fight one on one to the death.

She stepped out once more when the time came. A wind blew around her and she scanned the horizon. The Choir, that long hated enemy, lay beyond the distant mountains. However, the sword had become a comfort, a comfort, to Layla as she tightened her grip on it.

She whispered, 'This where it starts.' The camera pulls back, to show her looking at her comrades, who would all march toward their destiny.

Final Battle

On the ridge, the wind howled past Layla and past the battlements while she stood at the front looking down at the battlefield below. The energy of the central node of The Choir, a ragged, pulsating thing, filled her eyes. Storm clouds churned in the sky, lightning flashes piercing the jagged spires flashing an eerie green light upon the scene. The tension was thick in the air, not only in the heavens, but inside of her, too.

That left the others behind her crouched behind masks pulling the silents from grappling them as they were immune to the Choir's influence. Fewer now than once great the force they had been. But they were still here. Still breathing. Still ready to fight. Layla's loyalty and trust was spoken for but palpable, they waited in silence.

Her expression was unreadable—indifferent, her mind a tempest of contradictory thoughts. This was it. The final confrontation. They'd lost everything and stood on the edge of things more vengeance or annihilation. The weight of every life lost, every battle fought, the weight of leadership she once was so afraid of bearing, had all pressed down on her. But here she was, standing in front leading them one final time.

Above, a low rumble of a storm growl from the heavens, as the world itself seemed to know what was coming. Layla deep breathe in, closing her eyes for a moment to get back to center. There was an oppressive silence around her broken only by now and then a gust of wind blowing through the air. But it was not fear she felt. Not anymore.

She opened her eyes and turned to see the Silents. Those who hadn't looked in those eyes yet—the eyes that were visible—waited on them. Trusting.

Layla started, voice even, braced — though you could tell by the weight in it that it was everything they'd earned. "We've got nothing left from The Choir." But we are not broken." She looked each fighter in the eye, doing so with her gaze when it swept over the small group of fighters. That she knew what was at stake. "We bring the fight to those who cannot." We choose to fight because we do."

The sword ground her but she tightened her grip because she was rooted in the moment. Her words were unworthy, and their unspoken truths hung in the air, heavy, in the air. It wasn't revenge alone. It was about survival, about taking back what was theirs, about goddammit, not allowing anything like this to happen to anyone else.

And there was not hesitation in the silence from her comrades. It was one of solidarity. This far, this far they'd come, and they would follow her wherever she led them.

Layla turned before giving a last, sharp nod at the faces regarding her still present; the faces who had been by her side through every misfortune and every defeat. The signal to begin the assault, her hand went up. Shadows the Silents, cast into action, slid down the ridge, mouth the form of the heart of The Choirs stronghold.

The first crash rent a throaty hole in the air and set the amorphous chaos that followed. She had charged, she had lead the charge so many times before. A labyrinth of steel and stone lined the outer defenses of the stronghold, but the Silents moved through the enemy lines with dead precision, cutting like a well oiled machine.

Layla's blade sliced through the dim light, readily breaking the first wave of her enemies before her. She was surrounded by the heat of battle: the ring of clanging metal on metal and the energy blasts filling the air. Her trickle of sweat down on her forehead only brought her a little more focus on what lay before her; she had prepared for this moment, and now it was time to bring it all together.

The Silents moved as one, the attacks coordinated, clean. Explosions rocked the ground around them, sending debris flying through the air, but they pressed forward, undeterred. Layla's determination had not wavered; she'd fought too long and too hard to give in now.

As they pushed deeper into the stronghold, however, something shifted.

No warning, Layla felt pressure inside her mind like a vice snapping shut on her consciousness. She stumbled, and her vision blurred for a moment as the world about her seemed to shift, pulling her into a completely other realm.

With a glimpse from Tulk, the battlefield dissipated within a blink. Behind it stood the surreal and dreamlike scene. Thick fog lay in the air while inside her head, dismembered and confusing voices echoed all around her. With this, Layla blinked her eyes trying to clear her vision. The voices grew louder as they started to assault her head with those lustful, mocking whispers.

"You will fail. You will be alone."

The words echoed through her skull, harder and sharper than the last. Images went sweeping by her eyes—her comrades lying dead, their faces contorted by their tragic end. She saw herself standing alone on the ridge, her useless sword at her side, with The Choir's dark imminence looming over her.

Layla's chest heaved as she tried to hold herself anchored. This wasn't real. It could not be. But the voices. the voices were unmoving and frightening, ripping at her resolve, playing off every fear she had convinced herself was long buried.

"You cannot win. You are weak.".

Then and there, she hesitated. Her breath caught, and she felt doubt, cold and tightening around her heart. Could it be done? Was she the one to take the lead and emerge victorious? Or was it all pointless anyway?

"No," Layla whispered, her voice barely audible over the cacophony of voices inside her head.

She grit her jaw tightly down on the hilt of her sword, gripping it so hard that her knuckles turned white. The fog swirled around her, but she refused to be consumed by it.

"You can't control me anymore," she snarled between clenched teeth.

Screaming defiance, Layla tore herself free from the psychic attack, her body jolting back into the real world, jerked wide-eyed from a dream. Her surroundings snapped back into focus—the battlefield, the explosions, cries of war. And in front of her, a little ahead, an enemy soldier raised his weapon.

Without thinking, Layla rammed her sword deep into the chest of her enemy, reclaiming not just the fight but her head as well. The tide was turning now; now inside her head and outside her head.

She looked about and saw that her comrades continued to fight, continued to strive forward. Her cry against them had not fallen on deaf ears. They moved forward as well because they were inspired by the courage of their leader.

And now, the final fight.

In the distance the dark energy pulsed ominously from the central node of The Choir. Heart pounding, Layla stood at the entrance and looked up to the massive structure that loomed before her. This was the moment. That moment she had been fighting toward for so long.

Her hand tightened once more about the sword.

"This ends now," she whispered with resolve in her voice.

At her final look at the comrades whom she regarded as family, she took that one lonely step into the heart of The Choir's stronghold. Whatever lay in store for her came now. This was it. The final battle had begun.

Episode 22: Ultimate Defeat

A low buzz seemed to throb through the stronghold of The Choir, not quite a hum, just vibrating in Layla's bones with that constant purr. She stood at the entrance to the heart of it all, her hand up by the hilt of her sword, breathing shallow and tight. Beside her stood a small group of remaining Silents, all focused on the same target: the pulsing mainframe, the core of The Choir collective consciousness.

Huge black cables snaked across the sterile floor and walls, all meeting at a central pillar of light. It pulsed with an eerie, rhythmic glow, like the beat of some vast, mechanical heart. The room was smothering, sterile, cold; yet Layla felt the weight of the thousands of voices pressing down on her. The presence of The Choir wasn't just an excitement in the air—it was a suffocating force, like its tentacles wrapped around her head, squeezing harder with each step.

Layla swallowed hard, her muscles tense but eyes focused on the way forward. This was it. They'd reached the core, the place where The Choir was at its most powerful, its most dangerous. But also where they were vulnerable.

The sterile, mechanical nature of the place played into the battle waging in Layla's head. She had been fighting against The Choir for what would come to be an eternity, resisting their constant attempt to overwrite her will with their collective unity. Here, in the heart of the enemy, the battle for her identity was at its peak.

Every step closer to the mainframe became more difficult, as if she was walking through some kind of thickening air that hindered her movements. The room now seemed to be against her, with The Choir seeming to yank Layla back. Her breaths came faster now, but she pushed herself on. Her footfalls echoed through the space as each beat took her closer to the conflict she knew it was only a matter of time before she had to face.

All of a sudden, there were voices. They began faint and distant, whispers at the back of her head. With every step she took, though, they grew loud and more insistent until they roared into a hurricane in the ears.

Join us. We are stronger together.

Layla winced, clutching her head at the voices beating in around her. Air shivered before her, and out of the pulsing light of the mainframe, The Choir's entity began materializing. Not a single form but shifting mass of faces, voices, and memories, an aggregate of everybody whom The Choir had consumed. Eyes focused on Layla, and mouths opened in unison.

Voices bombarded her, filling her mind with pleas and commands and anger. They would not settle on simply breaking her resolve; they wanted to consume her completely. Layla stumbled backward as the weight of The Choir's collective will bore down on her heart, pounding in time.

"You are nothing without us," the voices hissed together in a discordant symphony. "We are unity. We are strength. Join us."

Layla gritted her teeth, trying to push back against the crushing weight. Her fists clenched around the hilt of her sword, but the burden of their words weighed as if lead upon them. The thing before the Choir stretched out like some writhing, monstrous thing- a personification of control, of all that cowed the mind. It pressed closer, and Layla felt her own grasp on herself begin to slip.

The instant Layla sank. Her mind becomes a blur of vision, and her sight flashes images of what lay ahead when some things were taken from her that she could not give up, and wrongs committed upon lives. The voices of the Choir grew harsher while answering the deepest insecurity she had for herself with irresistible force.

"You were never meant to lead. You can't do this alone."

The weight of their influence was like an avalanche, and she sank slowly to her knees. Dropping her sword with a clatter to the floor, she couldn't draw a breath against it. Layla squeezed her eyes shut, trying to make them stay that way. Her heart was sinking into the pit; the way it was filled by suffocating fear and doubt made it swell inside her chest. She felt herself slipping away, her will cracking under the pressure. The Choir wasn't just attacking her body; it was breaking her mind, her spirit.

This is how it ends, she thought. I can't fight them. I'm not strong enough.

But through the floating, buzzing jumble of words, a flicker of light. First faint, but growing brighter still, piercing through The Choir's phrases into her mind like a knife.

And then, clear and calm and so familiar, a voice, cutting through the noise.

"Remember who you are, Layla."

Layla's eyes snapped open. It was her mentor's voice; one person who had believed in her at a time she could hardly believe in herself. The words cut through the smoke in her mind and for the very first time in what felt like hours, Layla could think clearly.

She remembered. She wasn't just fighting for herself. This was for every one of them consumed by The Choir. For the Silents, for the people she had lost, for the freedom that The Choir sought to destroy.

Layla's hand closed over her sword again, the grip steady. She slowly stood up. The voices of The Choir faltered and the pressure gave way as Layla's presence came to full strength. With intent blazing in her eyes, she stood before the form that shifted mass of the entity of The Choir.

"I'm not afraid of you anymore," Layla said, her voice even, full of conviction. The words rang out in the room, slicing through the chaos like a knife. The monster recoiled, the faces contorting with anger and desperation, but Layla stood firm.

But even as it burst into a growing light, pushing back against that oppressive darkness which had seemed to yield to consume her, Layla began to feel a world stabilize and chaotic swirls of memories and voices to subside. The oppressive weight began to lift, and for the first time since she had entered the room, Layla had control.

With newfound strength, Layla plunged forward, sword alight with the spark of inner strength. The entity of the Choir lashed back, tendrils of energy whipping toward her, but the movements of Layla proved precise and powerful enough to cut through the attacking strands, fuelled by every strike.

The thing writhed and bucked, its hundreds of faces screaming in rage, but nothing could stop her. Layla was unstoppable now. She raised her sword high in the air, a radiance encasing her like an aura, and with a mighty thrust she plunged the blade into the central node of The Choir.

An energy wave went through the room as The thing shattered instantly, its voices gone in an instant.

Layla lingered in the silence, gasping to get enough air. The room was silent now, the oppressive feeling of The Choir silenced. She had won not only the battle against The Choir but also the battle for herself.

She regained her identity.

Episode 23: A New Song

The air in the heart of The Choir's stronghold crackled with tension, a dark shroud of despair draping Layla like some moth-eaten cloak. She stands at the center of the chaos; her heart pounding with the thing looming above her: twisted masses of darkness and fragmented voices. It is an abomination, a living specter, all hate and misery packed onto so many souls' shoulders. Every sound, every whisper spoke of defeat; her spirit was smothered beneath it. Layla's respiration came in heavy gasps as she fought with her lungs, forcing each breath through the crushing weight of the psychic forces that compelled her down.

Her fingers clutched at the hilt of her sword. Its blade was stained with residue and detritus from countless battles. Every battle she had faced; every wound she had suffered, it seemed a reminder. Comforting and burdensome at once. The metal felt warm against her palm, but it was not the weapon that gave her strength-it was the flicker of hope that sprang to life within her, a memory of the new code she had developed. It surged through her like flame, casting light into the dark crevices of her mind where despair would have taken root.

As the darkness churned around her, Layla closed her eyes and focused. The cacophony of The Choir was unending; they tried to drown out the determination welling up inside her. She felt the code deep beneath the surface, waiting to be released into its melody. It was time to take back her power.

"I will not be confined by your turmoil!" Layla yelled over the jarring noise. And with each word, she barged the fear that wanted to swallow her, anchoring herself firmly to the thought that she was much more than a pawn in this game. The faces of those who came before her—those who fought and lost— flashed before her mind, but their eyes shone not with despair, but with fierce determination.

They believed in her; now she must believe in herself.

And with renewed energy pulsating through her veins, Layla approached the complex lines of code with a sense of focus she had not experienced before. Now she could see it, this code coalescing around her-a tapestry of light and energy which would evolve into a ripened existence. Each line accounted for a bond; each thread of individuality was intertwined into one collective experience for all imprisoned in The Choir.

As she spoke the trigger words, the power began to throb in rhythm, echoing to the beat of her heart. It felt wonderful-it was a heady thrill of power flowing through her, and yet terrifying. The creature retired in surprise, lashing at her wildly as the darkness reached out to claw at the fringes of her determination. But Layla did not flinch, arms outstretched, face set in angry concentration.

The Choir unleashed a psychic blast, chaotic storm, shadows and whispers, straight at her. Strings of dark energy lashed out to grab her, pull her back into the despair. A sting from its assault struck her in the mind. Layla fought through the pain and clung to her focus. "You are not my reality!" she declared loudly, forcing her way through the pain as a beacon against the tempest.

Every fiber of her being screamed to give in and let despair envelop her like a shroud. She would not break, though. With each beat of her heart, she wove the code deeper into the heart of The Choir, feeling the pulsing energy shift from chaotic darkness to a vibrant spectrum of colors. The room began glowing, each color representing the individuality she sought to restore.

Layla felt the weight of hopes attached to her body by her allies' voices, urging her on. The faces of them flickered in the night sky like stars in her imagination, a constellation of dreams and desires all tangled with hers. "We are more than just voices," she yelled into the storm, her words flying sharp as a knife through the turbulent noise.

The creature responded instantly; its faces cracked and crumpled in on itself as it transitioned from rage to confusion. Darkness writhed, attempting to regain a hold, but Layla was a wall of solid resolve against the chaos. Vibrant colors of the code pulsed around her, living testaments of her strength and the bonds she had forged with those who fought at her side.

As the air shifted, Layla pushed on, pouring in the code straight to the heart of The Choir. Dark energies began to fade and fall away as shimmering waves of light fill every corner of the stronghold. Voices came up in harmony, a symphony of individuality rising from the depths of despair.

In that moment, Layla felt herself flood with triumph, but it broke immediately over her, leaving exhaustion in its wake. She could feel her body protesting, protesting this quota of the conflict laid heavily upon her. But she pushed through, every fibre devoted to this last act of defiance.

And with this last surge of will, Layla pulled the code completely into The Choir's heart. Energy spilled out and filled the environment with brilliant light that lit up the darkness. What was once voices in discord joined into a single melodic voice for each person who reclaimed their sovereignty yet still felt like they belonged with one another.

As the last echoes of despair dissipated, Layla fell to her knees, spent but grinning from ear to ear. The warmth enveloped her as if it were a warm hug, and she could hear the renewed voices pounding in her ears: "We are free. We are whole.".

It was then that Layla realized what victory truly is. Not by defeating an enemy, but hope in her heart has again come back. She had fought for herself but, in doing so, found herself fighting for every silenced voice in darkness and each lost soul.

And then, as the light kept burning around her, Layla breathed out a breath she hadn't even known she was holding. All that journey, all that pain and struggle: this was what it led to—a moment of unity, of healing, and of rebirth. The Choir, which had seemed a prison to her mind, Layla saw was now sanctuary of testament to the strength of humanity.

And in that moment of victory, Layla knew she had found a place among them, a beacon of hope in a world that had seemed so dark. The future stretched ahead of her, full of color and promise, new life for herself, and all whom she had fought to save.

Episode 24: Bittersweet Return

Layla stood atop a hill, where the morning sun warmed her skin as she gazed down at her town. It was another world, another world changed by the hard work, by the efforts that had resulted in that final key that resulted in victory over The Choir. Air pulsed with laughter and conversation, music drifting up from the streets, from people gathered in animated clusters. Layla's heart was swelling with pride and relief in an exhilarating mix of emotions swirling in her senses; there was weight at her side-she cherished, the blade still stained from the battle, a constant reminder of the struggles she had been through.

What he saw below was in total contrast to the stifling atmosphere that had once enclosed her life. Layla's eyes had been brightened by the sun-golden light shining on the faces of friends and neighbors now free to voice their thoughts, feelings, and dreams. It was a new dawn, and breathing it in, she savored the scent of freedom.

And one last glance across the horizon, Layla made her way down the hill of steps. Each step echoed with purpose as she moved through the throng of people, smiles and waves greeting her as if she were a lost friend come home. Familiar faces filled her vision: friends and family, those who had stood by her side in battle against The Choir.

Layla reached the heart of the village and warmth enclosed her. Mira, a young artist she had grown to know during the days of rebellion, ran to her, and tears of joy glistened in her eyes as she flung her arms around Layla's neck and said with a shaking voice, "Thank you for believing in us.".

Layla stepped back, looking Mira straight in the face. "This is just the beginning," she said to her reassuringly, with a calm and steady voice. "We have so much to create together."

Mira nodded her head as if in agreement, and a spark of inspiration lit the darker corner of her eye. The atmosphere was filled with laughter and urgent conversation, and Layla could finally feel hope once again as she watched people transform their community for good, finally free from the dark grip of The Choir-people finally discovering themselves, their voices singing out of harmony.

Entranced by the community center, Layla stood before a giant mural project. The walls were a riot of color, each brushstroke telling a story of individuality and collective expression-the final manifestation of the new freedom found in the community. She picked up the brush, and instinctively felt the familiar texture of bristles against the palm of her hand. She was unwilling and her first few strokes were hesitant but then urgently quickened into bold and expressive movements.

As she painted, lost herself in the process, let color on the canvas channel through her emotions. With every stroke, she felt lifting burdens of the past from her shoulder and dashing them down to be replaced with conviction that she was a part of everyone sitting across her. "Art is not just a form of expression, but it is our way of having a connection with one another," Layla whispered to herself, beating her chest hard with excitement. The mural became a tapestry of dreams and aspirations, a vibrant reflection of the community reborn.

Later, into the heart of the community, Layla stepped onto a small stage set up for an open mic event. Electric energy was brewing in the crowd and anticipation hung thick in the air as eyes finally turned to her. Layla felt the weight of hope laid upon her shoulders, and with deep breaths, drew on her strength.

"Let your voices be heard!" she exclaimed, her voice ringing clear and strong through the room. The crowd applauded and each of them, in their turn, told their story, expressed their fears and hopes. It was a tapestry of shared experience that told each tale as it emerged one by one but within its very fabric were woven solidarity and support. She listened with a heart swelling full of pride, hope--Layla watched as changes emerged in her friends and neighbors.

She sought a moment of quiet when the crowd was dissipating. She climbed a little rise overlooking the community. The sun set while she sat above. It cast long shadows on the ground and painted the sky with hues of pink and gold. There, she discovered a quiet spot and allowed reflection on the journey she had taken: the sacrifices she made, the friends she lost along the way.

She then fixed her eyes on a bench a little distance away, which had been put up as a memorial for those whose deaths had fallen to The Choir. She kneeled to the memorial, her hand moving along the cool wood surface with all the weight of sorrow in her heart. "I'll take your tales with me," she whispered forward, promising to keep going the cause for individuality and freedom in memory of them.

Layla's thoughts were centered on battles she and others had had to face, though she was still stuck in the darkness that had engulfed her in the past. But out of all the struggles she went through, she found herself standing stronger-an embodiment of resilience and hope. There, in her heart, lay the bittersweet flavor of her victory because it reminded her of her ghastly past while at the same time holding promises for a brighter tomorrow.

As the sun began to set, bathing the community with the warmth of the setting light, Layla went into the heart of the village to convene the community leaders for a meeting where full of enthusiasm, ideas flowed freely in the room.

"Let's have a festival of our individuality," Layla suggested, her eyes shining with excitement. The group broke into cheers as they nodded in agreement and started thinking of ideas-speeches on art, music, storytelling-and each added layers to the idea of a celebration of what was unique about them.

A smile flowered on her lips as she smiled, and with hope in her eyes, she waited for the future. The festival will be a celebration above all: symbolizing their commitment to newly attained freedom and identity, with a promise never to forget the journey undertaken.

And as their plan starts coming to life, Layla looks around at her friends and their allies. They all glow with hope. No, they shine like some sort of community reborn, every one of them a thread in this tapestry that is their existence together.

There was joy and laughter as Layla sat at peace; she felt so complete. She was a warrior fighting for the freedom to be free, but to others, she was a hope. In the road that was in front of them lay the shining possibilities and promise. Together, they would weave a life tapestry as a celebration of unity in individuality.

And in that instant, as they shared ideas and dreams, Layla realized the real triumph was not over The Choir but in what was made by the bond and the strength won from traveling hand to hand. And as the sun plunged on the horizon veiled with promise, Layla went on, her steady feet prepared for whatever the next stage would be.

Section Break: Rebirth

It was dawn-they so slowly opened to orange and pink, Layla sitting by the balcony embracing with both hands a warm herbal tea. The air was crisp, and Layla breathed it in, invigorating all of her senses as she took a deep breath and savored the moment. Sounds of laughter and chatter drifted up at her, like a comforting music, down in the community she was stirring to life. Layla saw children playing, neighbors greeting each other, the sun shining off bright houses that had once seemed miles and miles away from the dark, oppressive shadows of The Choir.

A mix of calm and resolve flooded Layla as she thought of the tumultuous way she'd traveled to get to this bright morning. Once-familiar faces were now full of renewed energy, freed from fetters that had long held them captive by The Choir. Layla allowed herself a small, tentative smile, but at her heart swelled with pride as she conjured images of battles fought and sacrifices made. Her sword weighed heavy, now splotched from every battle, and still at her side hung in full fury: the embodiment of struggle and triumph.

As the sun continued to rise, its warm rays painting the world with gold, Layla began to reflect inwardly. She opened her old leather-bound journal, that companion that contained all her hopes, fears, and dreams. Before her was the blank page that beckoned her to pour out her thoughts, struggling their way into her brain. She took a deep breath and started to write a letter to herself from back when.

Dear Layla," she wrote, her words streaming across the page. "You fought bravely against the chaos, and now it is time to embrace your strength." And this letter, written word by word, seemed another way of exorcising all that could be known about the suffering she faced. With each stroke of her pen, she captured her fears and victories and lessons learned along the way. Moments of her miserable past flash in her mouth between words—keeping silent, The Choir imposing isolation, and moments of second thoughts that nearly had consumed her.

Tears accumulated in Layla's eyes. She thought of who she once was, a young girl drowning deep into the darkness, holding out for that voice. Now, she faces sunshine on her face and the strength of the community enveloping her. Closing the journal, holding to her chest, it symbolized her journey towards self-acceptance and resilience.

With a clear head, Layla stood up and walked towards the community center, which now seemed a hive of creativity and support. Inside, she gathered her closest friends- Mira, Eli, and all the others who stood by her side during the darkest of times. They formed a circle, their faces very expressive and full of trust and vulnerability. Layla's heart ran over as they opened up their box and shared the stories that defined them, each strand raising the seams of bravery and ingenuity that their stories were cut upon.

Mira spoke first, her voice shaking. "I didn't think I could paint again after the choir silenced my spirit," she said, tears welling in her eyes. "But you, Layla, believed in us.". Our voices matter. Layla nodded, her own feelings welling up as she listened, attentive, nodding for him to continue. It was an air of camaraderie and warmth, bringing mutual respect, where the participants felt supported in expressing their thoughts freely.

The sharing circle reflected unity and strength in the bonds they developed through shared experience in troubled times. Each story was their testament to the healing power of community, and Layla realized her growth as a leader-a role she never could have imagined but welled up to fully embrace. As her friends spoke, she felt a swell of pride within her, a confirmation that together they overcome darkness into light.

After this circle, Layla went after Zain, who was the elder in this group. Zain was sitting under a tree with lush and colorful petals on it. The pets dropped softly, in the midst of whispering encouragement around them. Zain told stories of struggling past the community has experienced. Sometimes hope seemed to be so far that despair now threatened to take root. Layla listened, captivated by Zain's words, her expression a mix of curiosity and determination.

"Challenges will always arise but it's how we face them that defines us," said Zain, his voice as steady as it is calming. Layla soaked up the wisdom he spoke as if the words comprised all his years of experience in anchoring her resolve. It marked the significance of intergenerational wisdom-the need to learn from one who has withstood their storms.

Full of inspiration, Layla walked back into the community center. Standing before a large blank canvas, fingers tingling in anticipation, she will paint hope and individuality—the manifestation of her very dreams for this community. As she begins to sketch her vision, the camera caught the strokes—bold, free, and fluid.

The tapestry Layla had in her mind was of colors and forms. In every stroke of the brush, she felt the spirit of her community speaking. "Unity in diversity," she whispered to herself, her voice a gentle echo of her aspirations. On this canvas, her thoughts found a haven. Every stroke for her was a celebration of the various journeys that merged into one collective account.

As Layla painted, her voiceover wove the hopes for tomorrow: "Together, we are stronger. Together, we will face whatever challenges lie ahead." Those words jumped into her head, a mantra of hope to power her imagination. It was not only a mural of art; it was a promise to sustain an environment in which everyone could grow.

With every layer of paint, Layla felt herself unfolding step by step into her power. Community began to gather around her, drawn by the energy of creation. She exploded color into the blank page as rebirth, a declaration that became the fleshing out of their community.

As Layla retreated to look at the murals, a shadow danced upon her face as uncertainty gazed back at her from the memento. The mural in front of her looked young and full of life, shining with rainbows, but the obstacles that lay ahead seemed to echo in her head. Taking a deep breath, she stretched herself erect and with determination etched on her face, she said out loud, "We are going to meet whatever comes next together.".

The community erupted into applause, their voices rising in a chorus of support and encouragement. The strength of the community weighed upon her at that moment - the interconnected dreams shared together with her own. The mural would commemorate not only her journey, but the struggles every person who'd stood by her side well.

And then the sun dipped, marking the end of a day that had borrowed light from theirs. Layla stood amidst her friends, seeing hope and confidence niggling within their countenances. They had weathered a storm together, and now they stood on the brink of a new dawn-a rebirth kindled by the fires of their struggles and the beauty of their collective spirit.

Against the sparkling mural, Layla knew that their journey was far from over. It was the very first time that she would be comfortable with the unknown, believing that with her, they could face whatever came their way. Their community's rebirth was not a moment but a promise-to cherish its individuality while unifying in adversity.

Epilogue: Echoes of Harmony

The wind combs a tune through the trees; it's soft, and a gentle harmony that tells with a life once kept captive by The Choir. Layla stands at the meadow's edge, which at this time looks more prosperous than she ever could have known it might. Physical and emotional wounds lay there, but nothing defined people. Instead, they became symbols of survival, of resilience, of unity in the face of chaos.

Since The Choir had fallen, the community had changed. Everyone had found their own voice, their own rhythm, and with it, a freedom which in the old world would have been impossible to imagine. Art blossomed everywhere:on walls, in music, in the way people moved about and lived. That once-muted energy had been more than replaced by something vibrant and full of life, utterly personal. It was a mosaic of individuality and collective strength, because differences no longer divided but wove together to form something richer and more beautiful than a solitary whole.

Layla walked through the streets, now full of life and creativity. People greeted her with smiles, with small tokens of gratitude: flowers, trinkets made by hand, drawings-more of which were signs for the hope she had inspired than any true recognition of herself. Yet, in the end, she knew, it wasn't just her victory. Rather, it was the victory of every person who had dared to believe in something better, who had fought against the darkness within and around them.

But doubts crept in sometimes, when Layla began to feel what hardships would haunt them. The world was unsafe, and the whispers of The Choir were yet in the winds but did not have their stranglehold anymore. The people had learned to listen to the best voice: their own, trust themselves, and each other.

Looking out into town square, Layla felt a breath of the past lift from her. Replacing it was a quiet sense of fullness, like when sun finally rose in its fullness on the side of the mural she had been working on for months. Family and friends and strangers, who had grown to claim this place for their own, had filled in the blanks. And from it emerged a masterpiece—a testament to their journey together, those of whom an unseen but active force had, with a brush, begun to fight back. Vivid, bold, full of light.

As the sun was setting, spilling golden rays over the mural, Layla took a deep breath. She knew the road ahead was still far, and there would be more battles to fight and more victories to take, but this time the community, her community, was ready for whatever came knocking on the door. They were no longer mere voices lost in the cacophony of control. They were a choir of their own making, each voice unique yet harmonized with the others in perfect, powerful unity.

She turned to walk toward the heart of town. There, a circle of children played, and their laughter rode the wind like music. Layla smiled, feeling the sun warm on her face, and whispered to herself, "This is just the beginning."

And so the night closed over them, and the gentle hush of the wind that had been a soft melody grew into a song—a song of rebirth, hope, and a future they built together.

Afterword: The Journey Continues

Writing The Silent Choir has been an investigation of the fragile interplay between individuality and collective harmony, and of the incredible power that lies in finding one's own voice. Ultimately, though, this story was never and will never be about Layla and the battle against The Choir; it's about the resilience of the human spirit and its struggle to rise above the forces—both internal and external—against authentic living and the strength gained in standing together.

I often wrote Layla's story with the question of exactly what was freedom and self-expression. There are many types of "choirs" in our world-as there are in Layla's-and all such systems of expectations and pressures can leave us feeling like our voices don't count, that we must merge with the crowd to be safe. But this book was born out of a sense of a belief: namely, that we all have something unique to offer, and that it is exactly our differences that make the world a richer, more beautiful place.

Show through Layla's struggles and triumphs that individuality and community are not fighting against one another. Indeed, they thrive together. If we let us and those around us speak freely, create freely, and live freely, then something so much greater than anything one of us could ever hope to achieve by being is built. The case of Layla, just a lone sound stood up against oppression and became a leader who helps others develop their own voice, fortifies the notion that change starts with one but spreads through many.

I wanted to make it clear too, that it will never really end. Layla's story may come to an end, but the struggles she went through will change, just as they do in real life. Her community finally found its freedom, but there stand ahead of it new uncertainties and opportunities. Not merely an antidote to oppression, the Silent Choir was in fact an ongoing process of sustaining that hard-won freedom, nurturing creativity and individuality, building a world where people could flourish.

I hope this story inspires you to think about your own journey, the places of silencing you may come across, and the ways you can raise your own voice and those of others around you. That is one fight we share: for self-expression, authenticity - worth fighting for, no matter how painful or arduous the route may be.

Thanks for holding my hand throughout this journey. Layla's world is a construction, but the resilience, hope, and community she builds are all too real. There's still much to be done to build a world where everyone's voice is heard and we are cheered on as we fashion together a future that makes room for everyone to be as fully and unapologetically themselves as possible.

Let the journey continue with each of us, for Layla, for her community, and for us all. Let's take our next steps with courage and compassion, understanding we can do something special together.

Conclusion: A New Beginning

And so with the end of The Silent Choir, we are at a crossroads-not just in Layla's life but in the lives of all around her, too. An incredibly moving final chapter to this book: about transformation, about healing, about finding that voice again. But, more than anything, they are about new beginnings.

Once smothered under The Choir's suffocating control, Layla's world is now full of possibility and life. Her struggles were her own, and from them, she walked away forever scarred with the badge of loss, sacrifice, and the ache of finding herself in the midst of chaos. But it is in those battles that Layla discovers a strength she never would have known she possessed-and in that strength lies the power to direct others toward their own liberation.

But the story of Layla, and of those around her, is far from over. Libération is not something that occurs in one or two strokes; it is a process that will be continued on its long trajectory. The tales of Layla and her community represent a foundation of what is to come. The story of The Silent Choir has been that of self-discovery, unity, and resiliency, yet their themes will continue to evolve when new challenges and new possibilities are realized.

It is not just a victory for Layla, but that of all who were fighting with her, and for everyone who found the strength to stand up for their individuality. The Choir, in all its forms, are the various systems that silence or oppress us, and we face our own version of the force that Layla faces. Whether it is the fear of opinions from others, societal pressures, or the efforts made by outside parties, the fight for personal freedom is etched across every being.

The message that resonates through this story is hope—hope that no matter how entrenched we may be in our conformity, there will always be a way to escape. It reminds one that we all are never alone in this struggle and together we can rise up to overpower whatever desire to squash our truth.

And here at the end of the pages of The Silent Choir we remember our voices count. The apparently incoherent and insignificant little contribution from each one of us adds toward the final harmony of the world at large. Layla's bitter-sweet victory is, in itself, a vicarious victory that reminds each one of us to alter things-it's in our own lives, to start with, and then in our communities.

It's not the end of Layla's story, just as it is not the end of ours. Every ending is a doorway to new beginnings. In those beginnings is room for growth, healing, and to become more of who we really are.

Thank you for walking alongside Layla on this journey. May her courage inspire yours and may her triumphs remind you that even against insurmountable odds, the human spirit can find a way to break free.

The Choir is silent now. And in that silence, your voice can finally be heard.

With hope for the future,

Manpreet Bhatti